She was dreaming again...

"Miss me, Susannah?"

"No, I don't," she said, but her arms snaked around J.D.'s neck and tugged him closer. He felt so good and hard, a lean male with sculpted, taut thighs that fell between hers, not to mention knees that pressed insistently, telling her what he wanted. Then a delightful graze of warm, smooth lips— but the kiss burned.

"C'mon, say you still love me."

But she didn't. It was over between them. Yet he was breaking her resistance, and each time his lips touched hers, she felt more languid and insubstantial.

Susannah muttered, "I hate you, J.D."

"I can tell."

She'd become attuned to him, learning the idiosyncrasies of his body as well as those of her own, committing them to memory, just so she could drive him crazy with lust....

Suddenly she startled awake and her eyes blinked open. She'd been dreaming.

And just as before, her sensual fantasies seemed impossibly *real*....

Dear Reader,

Good girlfriends, annoying bad-boy boyfriends and my lifelong love of the American South all provided inspiration for this story. In *Naked Ambition,* and an upcoming companion novel, *Naked Attraction,* two best girlfriends leave their favorite men in the Mississippi Delta, only to be called home again to their lovers.

In addition to being great fun to write, this story also brings me very close to having penned my fiftieth published romance. For this reason, I'd like to take the opportunity to voice a heartfelt thanks to readers for enjoying the stories and for offering support over the years. Thank you so much!

Sincerely,

Jule McBride

Jule McBride

NAKED AMBITION

HARLEQUIN®

TORONTO • NEW YORK • LONDON
AMSTERDAM • PARIS • SYDNEY • HAMBURG
STOCKHOLM • ATHENS • TOKYO • MILAN • MADRID
PRAGUE • WARSAW • BUDAPEST • AUCKLAND

Recycling programs
for this product may
not exist in your area.

ISBN-13: 978-0-373-79447-8
ISBN-10:   0-373-79447-9

NAKED AMBITION

Copyright © 2009 by Julianne Randolph Moore.

www.eHarlequin.com

Printed in U.S.A.

ABOUT THE AUTHOR

Jule McBride is a native West Virginian. Her dream to write romances came true in the '90s with the publication of her debut novel, *Wild Card Wedding*. It received a *Romantic Times BOOKreviews* Reviewer's Choice Award for Best First Series Romance. Since then, the author has been nominated for multiple awards, including two lifetime achievement awards. She has written for several series, and currently makes her happy home at Harlequin Blaze. A prolific writer, she has almost fifty titles to her credit.

Books by Jule McBride

HARLEQUIN BLAZE
67—THE SEX FILES
91—ALL TUCKED IN...
226—SOMETHING IN THE WATER...
281—THE PLEASURE CHEST
355—COLD CASE, HOT BODIES

Don't miss any of our special offers. Write to us at the following address for information on our newest releases.

Harlequin Reader Service
U.S.: 3010 Walden Ave., P.O. Box 1325, Buffalo, NY 14269
Canadian: P.O. Box 609, Fort Erie, Ont. L2A 5X3

1

November 2007

EVERY TIME SHE SO MUCH AS LOOKED at J. D. Johnson, Susannah Banner could swear she felt his big, hot hands removing all her clothes, never even bothering to leave behind the panties. Even worse, the undeserving man had had this bothersome effect on her since she was only five years old, knee-high to a grasshopper her daddy had called her.

Yes, J.D. had started ruining her life as early as grade school, where she'd had the misfortune of first meeting him, Susannah fumed as she drove her compact car along Palmer Road, past Hodges' Motor Lodge. She then cornered off the main drag and into the back parking lot of Delia's Diner to hide the car so J.D. wouldn't see it if he followed her. She'd been young when she'd met J.D., and well, what little girl— especially one so innocent as Susannah—could have seen through a male as duplicitous as J. D. Johnson?

Years later, when Susannah was old enough, she'd fantasized about him for hours, a mistake that had led to hot-heavy sex and feelings of sincere regret. Not even in a proper bed, she reminded herself, her fury rising, but in the bed of his daddy's pickup truck.

Just minutes ago, J.D. had drawn his last straw, and she was still reeling. Oh, Susannah knew he hadn't been born with the sense God gave a gnat, but then what man had? J.D. possessed the devil's double-edged tongue when it came to sweet-talking his way out of bad tasting situations, too. And he'd been gifted with a singing voice that could charm the skin off a rattlesnake, and worse, the pants off any female country-western fan in America.

Susannah wasn't like those women, though, she thought as she headed toward the door to Delia's. Why should Susannah be impressed by J.D.'s good fortune, after all? Like everybody else in Bayou Banner, she'd known him before he was rich and famous. In fact, she was one of the chosen few who knew what the initials J.D. stood for.

"I just wish I hadn't married you, Jeremiah Dashiell," she muttered. It had been her biggest mistake. Tears shimmering in her soft blue eyes, she tossed one of her trademark oversize handbags into the corner that she and her best friend, Ellie Lee, occupied every Saturday morning for breakfast.

As Susannah scooted in after the bag, Ellie set aside a tented white reserved card written in Delia's calligraphy.

"Please forgive me!" Susannah began, scarcely registering that Ellie was still wearing sunglasses, although the day was overcast. "J.D. made me late." Susannah shook her head, making the ends of her long, wavy sun-streaked blond hair swirl around her face. "God, I hate him! I just wish I'd had sex with somebody besides him just once. But no," she continued, "I've always been faithful." She'd doubted that was the case with J.D., and now her worst fears had been realized. She blinked back tears. "Do you realize he's the only man I've ever slept with, Ellie?"

"Sure, I was born the day after you in the hospital in Bayou Blair," Ellie reminded. "So I've known you even longer than you've known J.D. And I agree. I think you should have slept with that banjo player, at least. Remember the hottie who played in J.D.'s band in high school? The one who looked like Justin Timberlake?"

"The one who called every time me and J.D. hit the skids?"

Susannah muttered, wondering how she was going to tell Ellie what had just happened. Thinking about the banjo player was a welcome diversion. She'd kissed him and let him feel her breasts, but that was all. "How could I forget him? Of course, three weeks after I saw him, I married J.D." She glared down at the gold band on her ring finger.

"You should have insisted on an engagement," Ellie mused, eyeing the band. "That would have given you time to consider the consequences."

"True." After his career had taken off, J.D. had offered to buy her a diamond, so it would look as if they'd been engaged, but Susannah had refused, since that would have ruined the spontaneity of their wedding night. Now, of course, their whole marriage was a lie. "You think I would have stayed single if I'd talked to somebody with a crystal ball?"

"Honey, not even Mama Ambrosia could have seen your and J.D.'s future."

The local fortune teller had a cabin on a meandering tributary near Bayou Banner. As angry as she was, Susannah could admit Ellie was right. Not even a professional such as Mama Ambrosia could explain the magic that still happened sometimes between Susannah and J.D. They'd even made up their own private language for it, with code phrases for lovemaking such as *scarves and cards* or *hats and rabbits*.

J.D.'s slow drawl rumbled in Susannah's ear, and she could almost feel his warm breath tickling the lobe. "What about a game of scarves and cards, Susannah?"

He'd proposed on one of those liquid-velvet nights the Mississippi Delta had made famous, when the moon was just right, and shadows on the surface of the bayou rippled like fairy wings, making everything seem like an illusion, including scents of forsythia that stirred in the midnight air as gently as the cream in Madame Ambrosia's darkest love potions.

Their prom clothes—his tux and her butter-yellow dress beside them—they'd been lying naked on their backs on pine needles, stargazing through the waving fronds of willow branches. With a voice as smooth as the inky sky, J.D. had sung the traditional song, "Oh, Susannah"—something he always did, since his family had come from Alabama—then he'd whispered, "I want to marry you right now, oh, Susannah Banner."

She'd smiled into blue eyes, threading her fingers in the dark hair of his chest, then she'd kissed him, his light goatee tickling her nose and chin. "You want to marry me right now?" she'd teased, just to hear him say it again. She'd never heard anything as sexy as his drawl, and everybody else felt the same way. His voice was smoky and mysterious, a low bass rumble that came from his chest and shot into a listener's bloodstream like a Cupid's arrow tinged with sex. "I want to marry you this very second."

"Why should I say yes?" she'd kindly inquired.

"Because when we're legal, we can lie in bed all day."

"Now there's a typical J.D. answer." She'd laughed. "Sex is never far from your mind, is it?"

"Does that bother you, oh, Susannah?"

"Your sex drive is the only thing I like about you, J.D.," she'd assured, although secretly she'd hadn't much minded his sense of humor, either.

She had been eighteen then, and since her parents had died the year before when their car crashed on the road between

Bayou Blair and Bayou Banner during a flash flood, there had been nobody left to stop Susannah from marrying bad-boy J.D., except her big sister, June, who was ten years older. And of course, Susannah had never once listened to June.

"Well, J.D.," she'd said reasonably. "All we have to do is drive into Bayou Blair and find ourselves a preacher and a place to get a blood test."

And so, by the next morning, they were husband and wife.

Back then, J.D. had been playing music in clubs around the tristate, and he and his band could haul equipment in nothing larger than a cargo van. Now he came with an entourage, and she was lucky if his publicist, Maureen, would even share his most current cell phone number. Susannah had never been interested in gadgets, but her traditionally decorated house was full of them at the moment—everything from new phones to fancy laptop computers and an intricate home alarm system she couldn't even operate.

"Susannah? You gonna have the usual?"

Delia's voice cut through her reverie. Thankfully Delia was the polar opposite of J.D. Nothing had ever changed the diner owner—not two divorces, or losing her mama to cancer, or having her last boyfriend run off with the librarian from Bayou Blair. Come hell or high water, Delia remained as steady as a rock. She was a little plump, with a pretty face that never aged, and she'd always worn the same tan uniform and white apron. As always she was unsheathing a pencil from a mussed bun of tawny hair as if it were a tiny sword. She pointed it at an order pad, ready to do battle.

"What are you girls having?" she drawled.

Susannah shrugged undecidedly, thinking that Delia had even looked this way years ago when Susannah and June had come here with their folks every Saturday morning. Memories made Susannah's heart squeeze. After her folks had passed, Ellie had begun meeting Susannah here every Saturday, keeping up the Banner family tradition. When nothing else in the world helped, smelling sausage frying on Delia's grill could usually soothe Susannah.

"I'm not sure, Delia..." Susannah forced herself to stare at the menu, only to notice her wedding ring and feel a wave of depression. "I'm not very hungry. Maybe toast—"

Groaning, Delia dropped the order pad into her apron pocket and planted her hands on her hips. "I should have known something was wrong by the crazy way you pulled into my parking lot. What did your devil in blue jeans do now?"

"Not a thing," Susannah lied, knowing if she opened her mouth—at least to anybody except Ellie—her dirty laundry would be hanging out for all of Bayou Banner to see. Of course, before J.D., Susannah's own mama had caused a few eyebrows to rise around town, too.

Still, the Banners had been the town's most prominent family, and Susannah had hoped to uphold tradition. However, instead of decorating the town square's Christmas tree or spearheading the Easter egg drive, she'd spent most of her time apologizing for her rowdy husband and his big-city friends, all of whom made her mama look tame.

Suddenly, something inside Susannah's chest wrenched, and she almost uttered a soft cry; she could swear her heart had done three somersaults and now, it was aching to beat the band. How could she get the old J.D. back? The sweet, gentle man she'd married?

If only her mama was alive! Barbara Banner would have known how to handle J.D. She'd been a delicate woman who read too much, painted in her spare time and was overly emotional and prone to indulge too many fantasies, the type to take to her bed in winters, and to get involved in dramas of her own making. Still, her advice about men was always on target. Realizing Delia and Ellie were staring at her, Susannah blinked.

"You sure you're okay, honey?" asked Delia.

"Fine," Susannah lied. Knowing only a hearty appetite would appease Delia, she added, "I changed my mind. I'll have the usual. In fact, you'd better add extra grits." As she said the words, her stomach rumbled. Like most Southern women, Susannah included, Delia had inherited enough mouthwatering recipes to open a restaurant. For years, Susannah had been begging Delia to share her recipe for strawberry-rhubarb pie, but Delia kept refusing, saying the ingredients were top secret. "I'll have my favorite pie for dessert," Susannah added.

For Delia, having dessert after breakfast showed proof of mental stability—it was as good as formal papers signed by the board of health—so she sighed in relief, then took Ellie's order and headed for the counter, saying over her shoulder, "I'm puttin' cornbread on top of them grits, too, honey-bun. That'll keep that miserable excuse for a man from scrambling your noggin. Yes ma'am, the only thing I allow to be scrambled in Delia's Diner is my own damn eggs."

Lifting a hand so as to display her airbrushed nails, Delia held her thumb and forefinger an inch apart to indicate the minuscule length of J.D.'s penis. "Johnson's johnson," she called loudly, just in case Susannah hadn't caught the allusion.

Susannah wished it were true, but unfortunately J.D. was hung like a racehorse, and he knew how to use every inch of his equipment. Otherwise Susannah would have divorced him by now, or at least that's what she told herself.

"You look like you've seen a ghost," Ellie drawled as Delia put in their order.

"I have. Of my own husband. Oh, he was always kind of wild. Everybody knows that, Ellie. I hate to admit it, but that's why I fell in love with him. I think J.D.'s shenanigans remind me of Mama. Remember how dramatic she could be? So full of life? How she'd race around town in that little pink convertible Daddy bought her? But this…" She shook her head. "He threw another wild party."

"That's nothing new."

"True." But the house they shared, Banner Manor, meant the world to Susannah, and one of her dreams had been to restore its former glory. She and June had grown up there, and despite its sizable acreage and isolated location, nestled in a grove of mature oaks, Susannah had kept living there after her folks were gone. By then, June had moved into town with her husband, Clive, and they'd had two kids.

So naturally J.D. had moved in after he'd married Susannah. They hadn't even discussed it, no more than they'd talked about having kids or sharing finances. At eighteen and twenty-two, respectively, passion had been their focus.

"What?" prompted Ellie, drawing Susannah from her reverie once more. "Did some cigarette-smoking guitar player burn another hole in the upholstery?"

Susannah visualized a nicotine stain left on her mama's favorite love seat, wishing it were that simple. She swallowed around the lump in her throat. "Do you remember how I was going to that two-day seminar you turned me onto, in Bayou Blair? The one about how to start your own business?" Because she figured J.D.'s new friends would only destroy any improvements she made at Banner Manor, and she wasn't going to have kids while J.D. was acting like a kid himself, Susannah was considering opening a shop, although she didn't yet know what kind.

"You went, right?"

"Yeah. I got back this morning, so I figured I'd stop by the house before I met you, drop off my bags and say hi to J.D. I mean, I've been gone for two days." It was her longest trip away from home since high school, and the sad truth was, she'd enjoyed it, except that the seminar had been in the town where she and J.D. had eloped.

"You found a house full of people?"

"You knew?"

"You just missed Sheriff Kemp. He told everybody in Delia's that he got complaints last night about noise."

"Sheriff Kemp? Was he in here flirting with Delia again?"

"Yeah, but he didn't ask her out yet."

Ever since Delia's boyfriend left her, the sheriff had been sniffing around. "How could he get a complaint about our house? You know how isolated it is!"

"Gladys Walsh drove up to the door out of sheer nosiness."

The woman was a known town biddy. "Next thing you know, Mama Ambrosia will see parties in her crystal ball and start communicating with busybodies telepathically." Susannah sighed. "I'm at my wit's end," she added, her throat closing with unshed tears. "J.D.'s a grown man. He ought to be thinking about settling down." At first, she'd enjoyed the parties, been excited to share J.D.'s new success, but things had spun out of control, and lately she missed the normal life they'd once shared. But now the stuff had really hit the fan....

"He's under pressure," Ellie ventured.

"I know," Susannah said. In the past six years, he'd become Bayou Banner's most celebrated native son, the only home-grown talent, and she and Ellie had discussed the issues related to his good fortune many times. Nevertheless, even Ellie's lover, Robby Robriquet, wouldn't hang around J.D. anymore, and those two had been as thick as thieves since birth.

"When I married him, we had sex every five minutes, and I was ready to start a family. Everybody said I was too young, but Mama and Daddy were gone, and June was married, and I wanted that life for J.D. and me. I figured he'd keep playing music on weekends and take over the bait-and-tackle shop when his folks retired to Florida, since he worked there all his life."

Instead, two years into the six-year marriage, J.D. had hired someone else to handle the shop, and Susannah had been trying to get pregnant. She and J.D. had even seen a fertility specialist, but he'd just said their timing wasn't right.

Susannah squeezed her eyes shut, recalling the day J.D. and his band had auditioned to be on a nationally televised talent show. They'd gotten on, then won, but only J.D. had been pursued by a record company; they'd insisted he work with a new band. Not that his buddies held a grudge about that. Everybody agreed that J.D.'s talent was special. Still, one thing had led to another, and there were rumors that J.D.'s third record might be nominated in the coming year for a prestigious music award.

"He's so full of himself," Susannah continued. "Like a stranger. And not a stranger I'd want to know." Sometimes after dark, she would sit in her car, in the driveway of Banner Manor, dreading going inside her own home. It was as if the world's worst forces were in there, fighting to claim J.D.'s soul and he was losing.

"When I got home this morning, the door to Mama and Daddy's old room was open. And you remember how I asked J.D. to keep that room off limits to his buddies?" Musicians, groupies, a cameraman and publicist were staying in the house, and more than once, Susannah had run into people in her own kitchen whom she'd never met before. "It's the one thing I made J.D. swear he'd do for me."

"I witnessed that conversation." Ellie frowned. "And that woman was there, too. You know, the tall, gorgeous one who looks like a model?" Pausing, Ellie added, "I think she'd be more attractive if she lost the military look. She's always wearing those heavy boots and flak-inspired jackets?"

Boy did she. "That's her. Sandy Smithers." She was with a group who'd come, supposedly, to help J.D. arrange music for his new lyrics. "Until this morning, I thought she was with that lanky blond bass player," Susannah said.

"Joel Murray?"

"Yeah. He's a studio musician." Susannah nodded, feeling sick. She'd never changed anything in her folks' room, and since their passing, that had comforted her. But… "When I went in this morning, Laurie—"

"Laurie?"

"Was in Mama and Daddy's bed with Joel."

"Laurie? June's daughter? Your niece?"

Susannah nodded.

"She's fifteen! That's statutory rape!"

"She hadn't slept with him yet. They were just… Well…she was wearing panties, but he was naked."

"The guy must be at least thirty. What did you do?"

"Shrieked like a banshee, tossed him into the hallway, then told Laurie to get dressed and wait in the car. After that, I headed for my and J.D.'s room—"

"And?"

"Oh, Ellie," she said in a rush. "J.D. was in bed with that woman Sandy Smithers."

"No!"

Invisible bands tightened around Susannah's chest and

she couldn't breathe. "Well, I must have screamed. I don't really know. I was in such shock. She jumped up, grabbed the sheet and ran—"

"She was naked?"

"Totally. By then, J.D. was up, and I said…" Shaking her head, she decided she'd never repeat what she'd said. Already the words were haunting her, and she had to fight the impulse to run home, find J.D. and take everything back. Just as in the past, a tender touch would make everything all right. Surely there was a reason he'd been in bed with Sandy. But what kind of excuse would explain that.

"Susannah?"

She barely heard her friend. "I told him I'm leaving him," she managed. "Among a few other choice words. I love him, but I shouldn't have stayed this long, Ellie."

"Well, you never had a choice."

"True." Susannah was his. And J.D. was hers. Even as kids, they'd recognized they belonged together. He'd been mean at first—tweaking her braids at school and trying to get a glimpse of her panties every time she climbed trees, tomboy that she was. Later, he'd played the big brother she'd never had, defending her honor. Then, he'd started touching her in a way no other man ever would, proving there was more to sex than the mere merging of bodies. Call it chemistry. Or magic. But a thousand men could walk past and Susannah's pulse wouldn't race, and her knees wouldn't weaken, and she wouldn't feel breathless and painfully aware of every sweet place she wanted J. D. Johnson—and only J. D. Johnson—to touch.

Just thinking about loving him sent a rush of adrenaline through her system. Tingles skated down her spine, her nipples peaked and suddenly, she was aware of her upper thighs, not to mention the ache between them. A slow, enticing longing made her shudder. The truth was, she could almost orgasm just thinking about J.D. Dammit, she fumed, he was supposed to be her everything—her lover forever. A father to the kids they were meant to make together.

"Falling out of love is the worst thing that can happen to a person," she whispered miserably. Could she get through a night without cuddling his hard, muscular body, or listening to his steady breathing lull her to sleep? Even now, when they were fighting, she spent hours craving the lovemaking they used to share, before they'd started growing apart. Her hands wanted to cup his broad shoulders, then trace over his pectorals and his washboard-flat belly.

Worse, with her mother gone and June married, there was nobody to give advice except Ellie—and Ellie had never been married before, either. Still, Susannah's marriage had ended before this morning. Sometimes the spark would ignite unexpectedly, of course. Flames would devour Susannah and J.D., and for a moment, she'd believe their estrangement to be over, only to experience heartbreak once more.

"Mama used to say the secret to love is learning to forget," she murmured. But now Susannah had no choice but to acknowledge all the things J.D. was doing wrong. An image of him and Sandy flashed in her mind, both naked as jaybirds.

"Where's Laurie now?" Ellie finally asked.

"I dropped her off," Susannah said. "June thought she'd spent the night with a girlfriend. Laurie was wearing an inch-long skirt, ripped fishnets, knee-high boots, and she had a fake tattoo on her thigh, of a skull and crossbones."

"J.D.'s a lousy influence. Did she realize you found him in bed…"

Susannah quickly shook her head, her heart aching. All these years, she'd suspected him, but now…

"Here you go, ladies!" Delia arrived, setting down two oversize platters. "Eat hearty. Those plates better get so clean that I won't have to wash them."

"Ellie!" Susannah exclaimed when Delia was gone and Ellie removed sunglasses and lifted her fork, only to use the tines to toy with her eggs. Where Susannah was tall and willowy with honey hair and brown eyes, Ellie had a square-shouldered, almost boyish build. Her jaw-length, jet-black, wavy hair was pressed right up against her peaches-and-cream skin, making her look like a forties film star. "Your eyes are more red, white and blue than an American flag," Susannah said. "You've been crying."

"All morning."

"I'm sorry! I'm so fixated on J.D. that I didn't notice. What's wrong?"

"Everything."

"I thought things were great. Your daddy's about to announce you'll be running your family's company after he retires next week, right?" Ellie was a shoe-in, mostly because she'd come from a family of n'er-do-well brothers—the sort of man Bayou Banner bred like fire ants. Ellie's brothers weren't reliable enough to run such an accurate polling service.

"Robby promised me that when Daddy made his announcement, we'd tell him about us. Then we made love all night."

Susannah slid the charm along the chain around her neck as she did when she felt worried. Ellie had an identical necklace, and both charms had been engraved with the words, *Remember the Time*. Years ago, on a rainy Saturday in Bayou Blair, they'd asked a jeweler to make them.

"Then what?" Susannah prodded. After Robby had finished graduate school, he'd begun working for Ellie's father, a man known around town as Daddy Eddie.

"When I woke up, I could tell he'd been staring at me while I slept."

"And?"

"He said Daddy's giving him the job."

Susannah gasped. "Lees have run the company since it started. And that was back in the eighteen-hundreds."

"Right. So I called Daddy. But he said it's true. Robby could have told me last night, but before we made love, he sat there listening to me talk about how we'd work it out, once I got promoted and he was reporting to me."

"Robby accepted the job?"

"This morning he said we should get married, and I should quit work and raise our family."

"That snake in the grass!" Susannah exploded. She'd set out to be a homemaker, but Ellie had gone to college and graduate school. "You got honors in economics and statistics, and all the while, you were running Lee Polls. Your brothers were in school up North for years, flunking out of their classes, too." Every single one of Ellie's life decisions had been made with an eye to running the company, but Robby had just started working for Daddy Eddie this year. "What are you going to do?"

Ellie's blue eyes turned steely. "Go to New York and start another polling business to compete with Daddy and Robby."

Ellie was leaving Robby *and* Lee Polls? It would work out fine, of course. Ellie had traveled more than Susannah, especially since Susannah had come to hate accompanying J.D. when he'd started playing to larger crowds. People had treated her like arm candy, and that had been a blow to her ego, invalidating her many years with J.D.

"Come with me, Susannah."

"To New York? To do what?" Her résumé consisted of a

high-school diploma and the two-day seminar she'd just attended at a hotel near the airport in Bayou Blair. She'd always planned to stay in Bayou Banner and raise a family.

"You could find a man," said Ellie. "At least you could say you slept with somebody besides J.D."

"Other guys never got Robby out of your system," Susannah reminded, still reeling. "But not seeing J.D. on the street would help," she suddenly added. "I can't divorce him if he's nearby."

"He'd change your mind for sure."

Yes, he'd start kissing Susannah, delivering those little nibbles which were almost as famous as his music, then he'd take off her clothes, undoing buttons with his teeth, murmuring sweet nothings all the while. He'd trail hopelessly hot, wet butterfly kisses down her neck, the ones he knew drove her crazy, and by the time her panties hit the floor, she'd do whatever J.D. wanted. It had happened every time she'd tried to leave him, which lately, was about once a week. "I hate him," she whispered.

"Divorce is too good for him."

"The only thing I want from my marriage is what I brought to it," Susannah said bravely. "Just Banner Manor. And it would do me good to have sex with somebody else. Anybody, really. Maybe even a few people," Susannah added, the idea taking hold.

"I'm going to sleep with everybody I can," Ellie assured her.

Imagining all the hypothetical studs, Susannah said, "They wouldn't even have to be very cute, would they?"

"No. The whole point would be to get our minds off J.D. and Robby."

"I can't watch J.D. pack his bags," Susannah admitted. "I'd feel too sorry for him and maybe have pity sex. He's the one who should move into Hodges' Motor Lodge." It was where all husbands in Bayou Banner went during separations.

"You have money. You're still handling J.D.'s finances."

She could write herself a check for the trouble he'd caused her, but Susannah never would. "I don't want J.D.'s money." She'd settle for the ghost of the man she married. She'd been so sure she was marrying a guy who would run a tackle shop his whole life, and who'd be a good daddy to his kids.

"We can share a place until he leaves Banner Manor," Ellie urged. "I'll lend you cash until he's out of the house."

It would only be for a week or so. "I hate leaving him in Banner Manor, even for ten minutes." Especially with Sandy there. Fighting tears, she told herself that the other woman was no longer her concern since she was leaving J.D.

"It won't be for long," Ellie said. "Your folks left the house to you. J.D. doesn't need it. Between a lawyer and Sheriff Kemp, all those people will be gone soon."

By then, Susannah should have racked up some flings and J.D. would be just a memory.

"I just wish he wasn't such a…" Pausing, she searched for the right words and settled on, "Alpha man."

"Him and Robby both. Alphas of the Delta."

Susannah almost smiled at the play on words, but her heart was hurting. Suddenly tires screeched outside. She and Ellie craned their necks to peer through Delia's window just as a late-model black truck swerved on Palmer and turned down Vine.

"J.D.," Susannah muttered. "He's going to kill somebody driving like that. And with my luck, it won't even be himself."

"At least he's not in that new boat," Ellie muttered.

Named the *Alabama*, the cabin cruiser was docked at a marina on the river. Given the wild company J.D. was keeping, Susannah had blown a gasket when she'd seen it, knowing that somebody would eventually was going to get hurt. "You're too cautious," J.D. had said. "You've got to loosen up, Susannah. Have a good time."

Like he did last night, Susannah thought once more, an image of Sandy's nude body flashing in her mind. "He's probably headed to June's. I told him I was going there, and that you were on a business trip, so he wouldn't follow me here." Her voice broke. "Oh, Ellie, what happened to him?"

"Fame. He changed, Susannah. He wasn't always like this. He used to be one of the best people I know."

Susannah's eyes narrowed. Suitcases were piled in the backseat of Ellie's car. "You packed already?"

"My flight's in an hour. I came to say goodbye."

Goodbye? Susannah stared at the corner of Palmer and Vine, from which her husband had just vanished. The intersection had been a landmark as far back as she could remember, but now J.D. was out of sight and Ellie was saying goodbye. Susannah was at the crossroad, too. She loved J.D. Still, she deserved a more stable life with a man who wouldn't betray her.

"J.D.'s obviously not home now," she found herself saying. "So…I'll run in and grab a few things."

"Really?"

Susannah nodded. "I'll come with you, Ellie."

A heartbeat passed, then the two women said in unison what they always had when making a new memory together. It was the phrase that had prompted them to have the charms on their necklaces engraved, one that had started so many sentences of their conversations. "Remember the time."

Already, both could hear the other saying, "Remember the time we were sitting in Delia's Diner? You know, the day we left J.D. and Robby?"

In years to come, it might well prove to be their most pivotal decision. "Remember the time," they whispered, eyes locking. Then they hooked pinkie fingers, shut their eyes and made silent wishes. A moment later, after leaving bills on the table, they headed toward the door.

"Ladies!" Delia called. "You didn't clean my plates, and now I'm going to have to wash them! You didn't even eat your dessert. Where are you going in such a hurry?"

"On an adventure," Susannah called as she opened the door.

And then she and Ellie linked arms and stepped across the threshold, toward their future.

2

Eight months later

"SUSANNAH, YOU'RE MORE FAMOUS than J.D.," Ellie teased, smoothing a hand over her black cocktail dress and looking around Susannah's restaurant. "And any minute now, you're going to get the call saying J.D. finally agreed to your terms in the divorce!"

"Don't forget your polling company has been just as successful. Besides, none of this would have happened without you and Joe," Susannah said breathlessly, her heart full to bursting as she glanced around the cozy eatery she'd opened six months before, then at Joe O'Grady the man who'd unexpectedly walked into her life. "When the foxhole shuts, the rabbit hutch opens," her mama had always said. Still, Susannah was nervous about getting the call she expected from her lawyer tonight.

At noon, when she'd spoken to J.D. for the first time in eight months, he'd said, "Susannah, come home. Come tonight. Now. We have to talk."

"Not after what you did."

"I didn't sleep with her."

"Liar."

"Listen to me, sweetheart."

Against her will, she'd felt his voice pulling her heart-strings. "Are your friends still in our house?"

Our house. She'd said the words, knowing Banner Manor would remain hers and J.D.'s even after he was no longer allowed inside. "They're not my friends."

"At least you finally realized that."

"I'll get everybody out."

That meant he hadn't yet. "Promises," Susannah managed to say. "I can't see you," she'd added, then kicked herself for even having considered it.

"Just do it. We're worth it. What about all the years we've spent together? Come to town. Don't meet me at the house. That way you won't see any other people. Go to the *Alabama*," he'd coaxed, picking up on her vulnerability. "Just you and me. No lawyers. No music people. There's a direct flight in two hours. I checked. You'll be at the airport in Bayou Blair by seven this evening, on the *Alabama* by eight. Just go outside right now and catch a cab to the airport. Don't pass go. You know we can't get a divorce."

It was just like him, spontaneous to a fault, showing he'd never change, but she'd begin to weaken, anyway. "I can't."

"You have to, Susannah."

"Why?"

"Because you're my wife."

For a second, it seemed the best argument she'd ever heard. "Say yes."

The one word—so simple but so complex when it came to J.D.—came out before she could stop it. "Yes."

"Eight o'clock on the *Alabama*," he'd repeated quickly. Before she could change her mind, she heard a soft click, then the dial tone.

For the next few hours, she'd watched the clock, her eyes

fixed on the minute hand until the time of the flight came and went. Then she'd phoned her attorney, Garrison Bedford, and explained that she was being pressured. When Garrison called back moments later he reported that J.D. now understood she wasn't coming, and had to agree to the terms of the divorce. He'd promised to sign all necessary papers and vacate the house by eight, which was when she'd agreed to meet him. Now Susannah was waiting for Garrison's final call.

Just a few moments ago, she'd thought it had come. She'd been called to the phone, but then the caller had hung up. Maybe it was J.D. again. Each step in the separation had been messy. For months, J.D. had tried to keep Banner Manor, if only to antagonize Susannah. "He's saying possession's nine-tenths of the law," Garrison first reported.

So Susannah had settled into the two-bedroom apartment she and Ellie had rented on the Lower East Side. She'd started scanning personal ads, just like Ellie, looking for hot dates, but then Garrison told her to stop, since it would jeopardize her divorce. She's also taken the first waitress job she'd been offered.

By the end of her first day at Joe O'Grady's, she'd realized that sipping sodas while J.D. played music at various venues had taught her reams about the restaurant business and booking acts. Within a week, she'd devised an innovative plan to rearrange Joe's restaurant, expanding seating capacity and revenue, then she'd doctored the pecan pie on his dessert menu by adding ingredients from her mama's recipe, which in Bayou Banner, had been as famous as Delia's strawberry-rhubarb confection.

"She's amazing," Joe had bragged to Ellie, not bothering to hide his attraction when both women dined in his restaurant. "Susannah's got a knack for this industry. She talked to our chef about the menu, and he's desperate to try all her recipes. She ought to open her own place."

"That's a great idea," Ellie had enthused.

"As soon as J.D. agrees to the terms of the divorce, I'm going home to Banner Manor," Susannah had reminded.

"You only have to supervise when you first open," Joe had assured her, having heard about her situation during their interview. "Somebody else can manage the business later."

"J.D. hired somebody to run his daddy's tackle shop," Susannah had admitted, wishing she wasn't still so fixated on J.D. Unlike Ellie, she'd found something wrong with every potential lover in the personals. They were too tall, too short, too smart or not smart enough, and as much as she'd hated to admit it, their only true flaw was that they weren't J.D. Not that it mattered, since she couldn't have a fling till the divorce was finalized.

"Lee Polls is being run by an outsider," Ellie had reminded, as she and Joe had continued talking.

"I'm a financial partner in other eateries around town," Joe had continued. "I backed an ex-chef when he opened his own place and hired a manager here, so I can spend more time downtown booking acts in my jazz club, Blue Skies."

Ellie had shown Susannah an article about the club. "You own Blue Skies, too," Ellie had murmured, admiring Joe's entrepreneurial skills.

"Because my favorite part of the job is booking acts, I'm there in the afternoons when people audition," Joe had explained. "Susannah, if you've got more recipes as good as the one for pecan pie, and if you want to open a place, I might agree to be a partner, and even bring in music acts."

Susannah had started to feel as if she was stepping into a fairy tale. "You're offering to back me financially?"

"I'd have to sample your menu first," Joe had said, his tone suggesting he wanted to try more than just food.

"If we can make money, I'm in, too," Ellie had said.

"Tons," Joe assured.

Ellie and Joe had continued talking about restaurant leases, health codes and liquor licenses, but Susannah had barely heard. She'd begun mentally riffling through recipes handed down by women in her family for generations. The idea of opening a Southern-style eatery like Delia's Diner was so exciting that whole minutes passed during which Susannah didn't even think about J.D. It was the first relief she'd felt, and more than anything else, that had spurred her on.

"I can use Mama's recipes!" she'd exclaimed. "Why, Ellie, you know how everybody always loved her vinaigrette-mustard coleslaw and barbequed lima beans."

"Her hot pepper cheese grits were the best," Ellie had answered. "And nothing beats her cardamom-sassafras tea and home-churned ice cream with fresh-crushed mint."

And so, Oh Susannah's was born in a hole-in-the-wall near the famous Katz deli on New York's Lower East Side, on Attorney Street, close to the apartment they were renting. Even the street's name had seemed fitting, given Susannah's ongoing long-distance legal battle with J.D. Putting her energy into the restaurant had helped her escape negative emotions, and she'd wound up using the butter-yellow and cherry-red color scheme she'd spent so much time devising for the kitchen at Banner Manor. The white eyelet curtains she'd dreamed about covered the windows, and mismatched rugs adorned hardwood floors. Short-stemmed flowers were bunched on rustic tables in mason jars.

A month after the opening, *The New York Times* had run a picture of Susannah, Joe and Ellie, their arms slung around one another's shoulders. The dining experience had been called "down-home elegance," and ever since, there had been a line outside the door. Delia's recipe for strawberry-rhubarb pie had arrived with a note that read,

> The article's pinned to the bulletin board at the diner. You and Ellie have done Bayou Banner proud, and your folks would be tickled pink. Seeing as my competition (you) has moved out of state, I'm hoping you won't hurt me with my own recipe. Just promise not to franchise anytime soon!
>
> P.S., J.D. got even crazier after you left town, if that can be imagined. Of course, since Sheriff Kemp finally asked me out on a date (and I'm going), I'll do whatever I can to keep your soon-to-be-ex-husband from getting arrested. But you must know: Mama Ambrosia came in for coffee, and she says trouble is brewing in J.D.'s future.

Later that day, Susannah's emotions had tangled into knots. Since the *New York Times* article was on Delia's bulletin board, J.D. must have seen it, which would serve him right. He wasn't the only one who make a name for themselves. She didn't want to rub his nose in her success, she told herself now, glancing around Oh Susannah's, but the man deserved some comeuppance. Yes…revenge was a dish best served cold, she decided with satisfaction, studying a slice of Delia's pie as a waiter passed.

Still, what had Delia meant when she'd said J.D. was worse than before? Was the gorgeous Sandy Smithers gone? And was there more trouble on the horizon, as Mama Ambrosia claimed.

Kicking herself for caring, Susannah reminded herself of all the holidays, birthdays and anniversaries J.D. had missed. Before he'd gotten famous, holidays had been fun. On Valentine's Day, J.D. had licked chocolate syrup from all her erogenous zones, and now, as she recalled the event, an unwanted shiver of longing sizzled along her veins, then ka-boomed at her nerve endings in a grand finale.

No matter how much she fought it, desire for him felt like a rope uncoiling inside her. Her hands were burning to grab that rope and climb, but it wound around and around her making her dizzy as it spun.

Now she was coming undone, imagining J.D.'s hands grabbing the backs of her thighs, pulling her close. His hips connected, rocking with hers, and his erection was hot and hard, searing her belly. Sensation suddenly somersaulted into her limbs, racing to all her choicest places, and tiny jolts of electricity shot to her toes like lightning.

She could almost taste J.D.'s mouth, too, which was always as sweet as cotton candy. Realizing she'd been swept away again by her own imagination, she thanked God she hadn't gone to meet him on the *Alabama* and groaned inwardly, reminding herself to think of her soon-to-be-ex-husband as poison. And as soon as Garrison called tonight to say her divorce was final, she was going to take an antidote called "sex with Joe O'Grady."

"I can't wait to hear Tara Jones sing," Ellie was saying, nodding toward the stage.

This was the first time live music was being offered. "Me, neither," Susannah managed, but in reality, she just wished she could shake off the aftershocks of her fantasy about J.D. The backs of her knees felt weak and her pulse uneven.

Clearing her throat, Susannah added, "She wants a low-key place to play on weekends, but I'm not sure I can stand to hear country-western," The last thing she needed was to hear Willie Nelson singing "Angel Flying Too Close To the Ground," or Johnny Cash and June Carter's snappy version of "Walk The Line," or Patsy Cline belting out "Crazy."

New York wasn't agreeing with her, either. Even without Sandy Smithers in the picture, Susannah might have run away with Ellie just to escape J.D.'s big-city friends. All their hustle, bustle and hype had been worrying her every last nerve. Now that she'd traded places and was living in their world, she missed Banner Manor even more. A new part-time manager at the restaurant was working out well, so technically Susannah could have toured the city some, but she just wasn't interested.

Ellie was taking to the place like a fish to water, but Susannah was still pretending she was sleeping in her big brass bed in Banner Manor. Oh, it was fanciful, but she'd strain her ears until she could hear willow branches brushing against the windows in tandem with J.D.'s breathing. A chime made out of sterling silver spoons that she'd hung outside would sound, then she'd hear a gurgle from a dam he'd built in the creek to create a nearby waterfall.

Sometimes, if she imagined extra hard, she could almost hear the familiar creaks of the old house settling down for the night, then the whir of crickets and splashes of gators and fish in the wetlands. Music of the swamp, her daddy used to call it. New York's sirens and blaring horns would fade away, drowned out by her own hoot-owls. More than once, she'd cried herself to sleep.

Realizing she'd been staring across the room at Joe, she blinked just as he glanced up from Tara, seemingly oblivious to the charms of the singer's enhanced curves and flaming red hair. After saying goodbye, he strode toward Susannah and Ellie.

"Don't forget," Ellie sang. "Tonight, you and Joe are going to celebrate the call. Cha-cha-cha."

"So much for my plan to have sex with tall, dark, handsome strangers," Susannah said nervously. Joe's hair was blond, and he was no taller than J.D.'s five-ten.

"The longer you put off sleeping with him," Ellie said, "the more attracted he gets. He's practically salivating! I wish somebody was that hot for me! Even Tara Jones isn't fazing him, and she's stunning."

"If it wasn't for Garrison making me wait, I'd have slept with Joe already," Susannah assured, not feeling nearly as confident as she sounded. Of course, Joe had insisted on doing everything but sleep together. He was kinky and inventive and made up silly love games, so Susannah figured it would be easy to turn herself into a real hellcat for him. It just hadn't happened yet.

"As soon as J.D. says he's out of Banner Manor," Susannah vowed, "I'm going to wrap myself around Joe O'Grady like corn kernels around a cob, so he can nibble all night."

"Make a corncob pipe and you two can really smoke."

Susannah chuckled. Joe had kissed her and fondled her thighs under her skirt while they'd been eating hot fudge sundaes at a soda shop. He'd role played too, pretending to be a cop arresting her, and a fireman checking for intruders, which had made her laugh. She felt something, too, just not the sparks she'd experienced with J.D. But that was just because Garrison hadn't given her the go-ahead, she reminded herself.

"Oh, don't look so anxious," Ellie chided. "All men come with the same basic equipment, right? How hard can it be to have sex with a stud like Joe?"

It would be easier if J.D. hadn't been her only lover so far, Susannah thought. "Sex is pure mechanics," she agreed, determined to be her own best cheerleader. "It's just a matter of knowing what to touch, for how long, and when." Still…what if J.D. had ruined her for somebody else? Maybe she could forgive him for being a lousy husband, but for ruining her sex life, she'd have to kill him.

Ellie suddenly murmured, "Joe sort of looks like J.D., doesn't he?"

"No! Joe's got blond hair and brown eyes, Ellie! And he always wears suits! J.D. never bothers with a shirt, much less a tie. He goes around bare-chested in worn-out jeans and cowboy boots. He's dark, too, from staying out in the sun too much."

"I'm talking about Joe's body type," Ellie persisted. "He's medium height and angular, with slightly bowed legs and the same bony cowboy butt. He's even got a goatee."

"That's what's in style now," Susannah scoffed.

"I just noticed," Ellie continued as if Susannah hadn't even spoken. "Maybe you're not going to be able to get over J.D., after all. Are you sure you want this divorce, Susannah?"

Susannah gaped. "You're supposed to be my best friend, the person I can turn to in a crisis. I started using my maiden name again," she added. "If there's any resemblance between Joe and J.D., it's completely coincidental."

"A lot of guys have flirted with you, but you picked Joe," Ellie countered. "His voice is like J.D.'s, too. I mean, not *exactly*. J.D.'s a famous singer, of course. Still, Joe's voice is gravelly and low."

"He's a man, Ellie! All men have gravelly, low voices!"

The argument ended because Joe slipped behind Susannah. As he wrapped both arms around her waist and pulled her against him, Ellie said, "I'll leave you two alone."

"Fine by me," Joe murmured huskily. His muscular thighs strained against the backs of Susannah's and she could feel the nudge of what promised to be an erection soon. "I can't wait for Garrison to call. Excited?"

Susannah's knees threatened to buckle. Ellie was right! His voice was like J.D.'s! Oh, his voice was pitched higher, and she'd never mistake it for her husband's, but there was a resemblance. Why hadn't she noticed before? "Uh…yeah," she managed.

Then she noticed Ellie motioning her to the phone.

Garrison.

"The call," she whispered, panicking. As soon as she spoke to Garrison, she was supposed to sleep with Joe!

He was pulling her toward the phone, but as they reached it, Susannah slowed her steps. Something was wrong, she realized. Ellie had turned chalk-white. Extending the phone, she whispered, "It's Robby."

"Robby Robriquet?" Ellie hadn't spoken to her ex-lover in eight months; no wonder she looked as if she'd seen a ghost.

Taking the receiver, Susannah brought it to her ear. "Robby?"

"I have bad news, Susannah. I just talked to Sheriff Kemp, and we decided it might be better if I was the one to call. Uh…we can't find June."

"My sister?" As Susannah's fingers curled more tightly around the receiver, she visualized Sheriff Kemp on the doorstep of Banner Manor years ago. Clad in a tan uniform, he'd kept his hands in front of him, stiffly holding his hat. "We need to go inside and sit down, honey," he'd said. "It's about your mama and daddy." Susannah's whole body froze. "What's happened to June?"

"No…not June."

Relief was short-lived. Was the call about June's husband, Clive? Or one of her nieces, Laurie or Billie-Jean?

Before Susannah could ask, Robby continued. "June's fine, but we were hoping to track her down before we called you."

"J.D.?" The truth hit her with the power of a freight train. They'd been looking for June, so she could provide Susannah comfort. A cry tore from Susannah's throat, and vaguely she wondered if this was how Mama Ambrosia saw things in her crystal ball not really seeing them at all, but only feeling them deep down in her bones. A hand shot to her neck, and her fingers closed around the engraved charm that lay against her skin.

"I'm sorry, Susannah," Robby was saying. Had he continued talking all this time?

"There was an explosion on the *Alabama* around eight o'clock. An attendant at the marina saw him onboard. The coast guard's bringing what's left of the boat up, but it'll take a few days. Until then, we won't know whether it was mechanical failure, a fire in the galley or the generator. The boat blew sky high, then sank just as fast.

"Because of all the legal goings, on between you and J.D., Garrison's here. J.D. left everything to you. Earlier today, he refused to sign any divorce papers, saying you were his beneficiary. You need to catch the first plane you can. Ellie, too. It would be good if she traveled with you."

"He wanted me to meet him on the boat at eight," she said.

"Oh, no," Robby whispered.

The thought hung in the air. Had J.D. caused the explosion because she hadn't shown up? But no…he may be wild, but he wasn't suicidal. Maybe he was okay. Maybe…

"He's gone, Susannah."

Her consciousness seemed to leave her body. She was floating away, high above the room, staring down at herself as if she were having an out-of-body experience. "I'm on my way," she managed, but the words sounded foreign, as if a stranger had spoken them. It felt as if she were inside a vacuum. From somewhere far off, Tara Jones had started singing one of the last songs Susannah needed to hear, "Precious Memories."

"That publicist, Maureen, keeps asking me about arrangements," Robby was saying. "I guess she's bringing camera crews here. Would it help you if I talked to folks at the funeral home before you get home? Or do you want—"

Camera crews? This was a private matter. "Please," she murmured. She couldn't face this without help. Even then, she wasn't sure she could handle this. "Get those people out of my house," she whispered. "Especially that woman Sandy Smithers. Get her out."

"I will," Robby promised.

Somehow she said goodbye and hung up. The color was still gone from Ellie's face. "J.D.?" She asked hoarsely.

Woodenly, Susannah repeated what Robby had said.

"I'll come with you," Joe said, pushing hair from Susannah's eyes when she looked at him.

Had she really considered sleeping with this man? Joe O'Grady was comparable, but she'd known J.D. since she was five years old. Now J.D. was gone and Joe was all she had, and yet, she only wanted J.D. It was wrong, but suddenly she didn't even care about all the mistakes J.D. had made, including sleeping with Sandy Smithers. "I wish I'd never left Bayou Banner," she tried to say, but no words came out.

"The manager can watch the restaurant," Joe said. "I'll help you pack."

But her dresses were still hanging where they belonged, sandwiched between the cowboy shirts she'd always starched for J.D. although he'd never bothered to wear them. No doubt, her shoes were still in the over-the-door rack. The lefts and rights had probably been switched by J.D., something that always made him laugh because if she was sleepy enough, she'd put her shoes on the wrong feet.

"I have to go alone."

"You need somebody with you," Joe persisted.

She'd have Ellie, Robby and people in her community

who'd known her all her life. Otherwise, she wanted to be alone with anything J.D. had left behind, his effects and memories. Didn't Joe understand? Could anyone? J.D.'s death felt even more private than all the things they'd shared in bed.

Would she really never feel his lips crushing down on hers again? Or the damp, hot spear of his tongue as it plunged into her mouth? Or his huge hands as they glided down her belly, then arrowed between her thighs, stroking and building fiery heat? A whimper came from her throat she imagined his biceps—bulging with corded muscles, shot through with visible veins—wrapping around her and squeezing.

Due to the exertions of performing on stage, J.D. always worked out, even when he was partying too hard, so he was ribbed top to bottom. She could smell the strangely sweet, musky scent of his sweat, and she wanted to shut her eyes and revel in the feeling of its dampness against her own skin. Right now, she needed J.D. more than ever. Only he could comfort her, but that was impossible. He was gone!

She'd been in denial. She'd never get over him, no matter what horrible things he'd done, but now she had no choice. "Maybe in a few days," she forced herself to say. "Let me go down first, Joe…see what's going on. After the funeral, maybe then…"

"I should come now." His eyes were probing hers. All along, he'd thought she was ready to become his lover. She'd thought so, too. But it was a lie. She searched her mind, hoping she hadn't led him on, but how could she be expected to explain emotions to Joe that she hadn't yet admitted to herself? And besides, she wasn't sure how she felt. She couldn't gauge the compass of her heart tomorrow. Although she hadn't seen him for months, J.D. was her husband.

Joe seemed to respect that. "We'll talk every day?"

"Yes," she agreed numbly, confused but unable to cope with pressures. Would she have called off the divorce? Refused to sign legal papers? A whimper escaped her throat. If she'd stayed home, maybe J.D. would be alive.

J.D. had still wanted her, too! Of course he did! As Joe leaned closer, brushing his lips to her cheek, only one thought raced through her mind—he wasn't J.D. And then, suddenly, J.D. seemed impossibly close. She sensed his presence. Was it his ghost? His spirit?

She was far too practical to believe in apparitions, but she whirled around, anyway, glancing toward the white curtains covering the window. But no...it was only her imagination. She could swear he'd been right outside, though, on the other side of the glass. Shaking her head, she realized she was experiencing shades of her mama, who'd had a reputation for possessing a fanciful mind. Susannah's eyes searched the street, then settled on the name of her restaurant, emblazoned across the glass of the door. Fingers of twilight touched golden letters that spelled, *Oh Susannah's*, but she saw nothing more.

Silently she cursed herself for naming the business after a song J.D. had sung to her so often. More than life, she wanted to hear his husky voice again.

And she could, but only on the CDs he'd left behind.

3

IN THE LIVING ROOM OF Banner Manor, Susannah quit sorting
J.D.'s unanswered fan mail, losing herself to his music, feeling
unable to pick up the phone when it rang. *Oh, Susannah,
don't you cry for me. I've come from Alabama with a banjo
on my knee…*

She rarely drank. J.D. always jokingly said she stayed as
dry as burned toast in the Sahara, but now she took another
sip of brandy, wishing it would blunt the pain. Maybe she
should have chosen one of J.D.'s stronger spirits, the whisky
or gin. Either way, the most lethal spirit remained J.D.
himself, since memories of him were everywhere.

She finally lifted the phone and pressed Talk, figuring it
was either Ellie, June or Joe, they'd called daily since the
funeral two weeks ago. Of course, Ellie mostly wanted to talk
about whether Susannah had run into Robby. Seeing him had
made her best friend start obsessing about her relationship
again. "You don't have to treat me like an invalid," Susannah
said before the caller could speak. "I'm fine."

"Not according to my crystal ball. So, honey, if you care
about your future, you'd better not hang up on me."

It was Mama Ambrosia, the only other person who'd been
calling. "You again!" Susannah looked beyond the open living
room windows, glancing past French doors that led to a patio

beyond, then she took in J.D.'s guitar picks, which were strewn across the fireplace mantle. "Didn't I ask you not to call again?"

"Now, darlin', you've never come to see me, and I know you distrust my craft," Mama Ambrosia began. A large powerhouse of a woman, she prattled in a voice made deeper by the hand-rolled cigarettes she chain-smoked. "But your mama trusted me. J.D., too. He and I go back quite aways, which must be why his vibrations are so strong. All night long, I've been getting big ol' shivers."

"Pardon me for saying so, but you're crazy, do you know that? I don't believe in ghosts—I already told you that—so I hope you don't intend to restart the conversation we had the last time you called, which was only—" Susannah looked at the clock on the mantle "—twenty minutes ago."

"Crazy?" countered Mama Ambrosia. "So some say. But I'll remind you, missy, they said the same about your mama at times. Just like J.D., she was a handful, prone to daydreaming. And it's high time you admit you inherited her genes."

"Only the good ones," Susannah assured her.

Previously, Mama Ambrosia had claimed J.D. had been a regular customer, visiting often to hear his fortune, and since she'd divulged facts only J.D. could know, Susannah believed her. Try as she might, Susannah couldn't squelch the surge of hope she felt, either, when Mama Ambrosia called as if she might connect with J.D.'s spirit and say goodbye. Not that she and J.D. could resolve their differences, but still, she'd feel better. Despite being characteristically pragmatic, she found herself prompting, "You said you felt a shiver. What exactly does that mean?"

"That he's in trouble, Susannah."

"He's in far worse than that," Susannah pointed out, taking

another big swig of brandy. She'd scattered her almost-ex's ashes to the four winds. Determined to feel no more pain, she squared her jaw and drank some more, but the hot taste of alcohol only reminded her of J.D.'s kisses. Her throat was scratchy from crying, and the booze soothed it as the syrupy warmth slid slowly downward, burning all the way to her belly. It curled like a ball of fire and felt so good that she knocked back yet another drink, sighing when the scalding heat slid through her veins.

"He's in trouble on the other side," Mama Ambrosia clarified ominously, bringing Susannah back to reality. *The reality of non reality,* she thought, since Mama was clearly as crazy as a loon.

"If he'd caused as much trouble there as he caused in life, I don't doubt it," conceded Susannah, as if this were the most normal conversation in the world. "Maybe he and the head honcho of the underworld are fighting over who gets to hold the scepter or sit on the throne." She realized she must be feeling the effects of the alcohol when she found herself imagining J.D. gripping a pitchfork and wearing a skin-tight red suit that showed off his cowboy butt. Already he possessed the right style of goatee and mustache, not to mention a devilish glint in his eyes.

"Now, now," Mama Ambrosia chided. "You still love him, and that's why I'm calling. Even if you won't admit it, my crystal ball told me so. Besides, I'm morally bound as a fortune-teller to alert you to your dismal cosmic situation."

Yes, Mama was definitely certifiable. "My cosmic situation?"

"Expect a visitation."

Susannah was starting to feel like a parrot. "A what?"

"Visitation. As in when somebody visits."

Susannah could only shake her head. "I know what a visitation is."

"Then why did you ask?"

Not bothering to answer, Susannah said, "A visitation from whom?"

"The dearly departed who was your dearly beloved."

"Very doubtful." Thankfully, her call waiting beeped just then. "Sorry, I really should get the other line," Susannah said, trying to muster an apologetic tone. She was almost as mad at J.D. for dying as she was at all his other transgressions combined, so Mama Ambrosia's wild claims weren't helping her mood. "The last thing I need is a visitation from J.D.," she said. "And if I got one, I might just kill him all over again." God only knew J.D. deserved a fate worse than death for the mess he'd made of their lives.

"Whatever. And the other man on the other line," Mama Ambrosia said, "is the one you dated in New York. I saw him in my crystal ball, too, so I'll let you go."

Susannah couldn't help but ask, "Do you really have a crystal ball?"

"I used to, but it broke," Mama Ambrosia returned sadly. "This new one's plastic, but don't worry, it works just as well. Now answer Joe's call, darlin'."

Susannah was startled to hear his name, but probably, Ellie had mentioned Joe to someone at Delia's Diner when she was in for the funeral, and that's how Mama had heard it. Sighing, Susannah clicked the other line. "Hello?"

"Are you thinking about me?"

"Joe. It really is you."

"Who were you expecting?"

J.D. Determined not to let Mama Ambrosia fill her mind with otherworldly impossibilities, Susannah pushed away the thought. "You," she said. He wasn't even close to ghostly. He was solid and real, and his persistence kept reminding her that life was meant for the living. Suddenly she added, "*Where are you?*" It sounded as if he were right next door.

"Home. I just came from your restaurant. Tara's packing in people, and a guy from Chicago came by to see if she wanted to do a gig there tomorrow, which she is."

"Good." She paused, the idea that Joe was actually in Bayou Banner flitting through her mind. "We really do have a strong connection. Are you sure you're not next door?"

"I wish. But what if I come tomorrow? Ellie gave me her key in case you say yes and are out when I get there. She said there's a direct flight to Bayou Blair in about two hours."

So, Ellie was still playing matchmaker. "Please let me stay and help," she'd begged right after the funeral.

"You don't need to be around Daddy Eddie and Robby," Susannah had argued. "June and my nieces are going to help me, and besides, your business needs you."

"Then promise you'll let Joe come stay with you," Ellie had urged. "You need to try, at least. Let him comfort you."

"I'll think about it," Susannah had promised.

In the meantime, Susannah's new manager was using her boss's absence to shine, so Susannah had been able to remain in Bayou Banner roaming the grounds and sorting through J.D.'s belongings. She'd been listening to his CDs, too, although they made her ache, body and soul.

The soft, melodic songs on his first collection, *Delta Dreams*, had been composed with guitars, harps and flutes. *Welcome to My Town* contained humorous songs about Bayou Banner—"Dining with Delia," "When I left my Wife For Hodges' Motor Lodge," and "Sheriff Kemp's Blues." *Songs for Susannah* was the most recent album, and Susannah still couldn't listen to it without crying. Coordinators for the award ceremony had called; J.D. had been nominated, and they wondered if she'd accept the award if he won. Susannah had said yes, so she had to return to New York in a few days.

Thankfully, Robby had arranged the funeral, then held photographers and reporters at bay, as well as the publicist, Maureen, who'd arrived clad in black, crying louder than the bereaved, including Susannah's in-laws who'd come from Florida. J.D.'s parents and Susannah's real friends had wrapped around her like a security blanket, and the music had been perfect. The church organist played "Amazing Grace" and "Will the Circle Be Unbroken," songs that comforted Susannah even now.

At the river, near where the *Alabama* had sunk, she'd cast J.D.'s ashes to the wind. Cremation wasn't what anyone would have chosen, but the explosion made burial an impossibility. After the funeral, Sheriff Kemp had handed Susannah the only items the coast guard found—a Saint Christopher's medal she didn't recognize. The only saving grace was that Susannah's niece, Laurie, had straightened up overnight. She'd foregone her temporary tattoos, trashy clothes and blue hair coloring, and she was now dressing like a model citizen.

Due to the illogical nature of grief, Susannah had wound up stuffing J.D.'s silly old lumberjack hat into her pocketbook the day of the funeral, and she'd held it in both hands during the service. She'd always hated the hat, which was made of red-and-black-plaid flannel with oversized ear flaps. And because she thought it looked ridiculous on J.D., he'd always worn it to provoke her.

Now she'd taken to wearing it and dressing in his shirts since she could still detect his scent. She'd then wander aimlessly in her own house, sometimes plucking J.D.'s guitars, although she could play only the few songs he'd taught her.

Realizing she'd drifted, her fingers tightened around the

phone receiver. "I'm sorry," she murmured, putting Joe on speaker phone, so she could put down the receiver and drink her brandy. "What did you say?"

"I said I'm worried." His voice floated into the air, husky with concern. "Uh...how much are you drinking, if you don't mind my asking?"

She leaned toward the phone. "Just some brandy. Why?"

"You sound...a little funny."

"You're on speaker. Maybe that's why."

He offered a noncommittal grunt.

Thankfully the brandy was starting to blunt the pain, so she took another sip. "Sorry," she apologized again. "It's hard to be here..."

"Then don't wait for the awards ceremony to come back. Or let me come there. I want to hold you, Susannah."

He sounded so close. "I know," she managed. But she needed to be alone. She'd lost her folks as suddenly as J.D., and now Banner Manor seemed full of ghosts. More so, since storms were rocking the bayou.

Banner Manor lacked central air, and although there were window units, Susannah kept opening the windows. Outside, shadowy trees came alive at night, and alone in the dark, in the bed she'd shared with J.D. for years, she'd awaken in a cold sweat, hearing spooky sounds, then jumping from bed and heading for the window. She'd stare at the lightning, letting rain splash her cheeks like tears. And sometimes, she could swear she saw intruders on the lawn, but no one was there.

Back in bed, she'd shut her eyes and let scents from summer foliage transport her to recollections of physical pleasure she and J.D. could never share again. She'd cup her own breasts, imagining J.D. was touching her, then glide a hand down her belly and between her legs. Slowly she'd stroke, twining her fingers into her own soft curls until, in a haze of half sleep, she'd believe J.D. was touching her. Dampness would flood her and she'd arch, lifting her hips from the mattress just as she felt his tongue circle the shell of her ear. As she climbed higher, squeezing her eyes shut, she'd press her fingers inside, pretending they were J.D.'s hard cock, and then she'd hear his seductive whisper. "Oh, Susannah, how about a little magic? Do you want to play a game of scarves and cards? Hats and rabbits?"

Suddenly, she blinked, realizing Joe was still talking. "Uh...what?"

"I asked if your sister, June, had been there today."

"Not today." Susannah leaned toward the phone once more as she took another sip of brandy. "Her husband's folks came in for the funeral and wound up staying, so she's busy. And anyway, I've got things under control."

"Do you?"

"Sure," she said, but grief had overwhelmed her. Hours passed, during which she was lost to memories and couldn't fully account for time. Everything felt unreal, like she was watching a movie, or reading a book. She kept expecting J.D. to jump out from behind a curtain and tell her this was a big joke.

"If you really don't want me to keep you company, Tara asked me to go to Chicago with her. Just as friends, of course," Joe clarified. "She thinks I can help her negotiate a better deal with the club owner if her audition works out."

"That's sweet of you..."

"But?"

"Oh, I do miss you, Joe," she admitted. Dammit, Ellie was right. Susannah needed to let go of what was no longer possible. J.D. was never coming back, no matter what Mama Ambrosia said. "If you go, will you be back for the awards ceremony?"

"Sure. But right now, my bags are packed and by the door, and I wish you'd let me come see you. Wondering when I'll see you again is torture. When I shut my eyes, I have a vision of you that just won't quit, Susannah. Right now, I can picture every inch of you. I love your body, how soft your eyes look. I can feel your arms around my neck, your long legs gliding against mine…."

She swallowed guiltily. "I know, Joe—"

"No you don't," he interjected, sounding frustrated. "Give us a try. That's all I'm asking. I know you want me. And I want you. Your mouth's so hot." Words were coming in a flood now. "I can't wait to cover it with mine again. I want to crush your lips, feel my tongue inside."

His voice caught and his breath turned shallow. "I…think about your breasts. How they move under your top, Susannah…just like your hips when you walk on those mile-long legs. Sometimes, when you're in the walk-in cooler at your restaurant, I notice your nipples get tight under your shirt." Sucking in an audible breath, he said, "Susannah, I get hard just thinking about you, about the things we've already shared…."

"I know. I—"

"No you don't," he repeated. "He's gone, Susannah. And I don't want to hurt you or sound mean, but you were breaking up with J.D., anyway. You and your husband had been separated the better part of the year. I know you're grieving, but it's not right for you to be alone. Not when so many people care about you. Let me come there now. Or…"

"Or what?"

"I can't keep waiting, Susannah."

"I'm not trying to hurt you," she said. But she was, wasn't she? He wasn't trying to pressure her, but he wanted her, and she was so lonely. Definitely, she wasn't used to not having a man. It had been so long…

"Okay," she murmured, the brandy thickening her speech. "Come to Bayou Banner now, and we can fly back to New York together in a few days for to the awards ceremony."

"I'll be there before you know it," he said quickly.

Suddenly all her deepest recesses ached. God, how she craved to feel strong arms wrapping tightly around her back, and a man's rock-hard, hairy chest pressing against her breasts. She yearned to feel the heat of his searing, blistering mouth when it covered her lips. Already she could feel his thighs straining against hers. She deserved relief from all this sadness and grief. She deserved release.

"I'm on my way," he said. And then, as if afraid she might change her mind, he whispered a quick goodbye and the line went dead.

As the dial tone filled the air, she recradled the receiver and started. Something sounded by the window! Her feet moving of their own accord, she crossed swiftly to the French doors and stared into the darkness. "Nothing," she whispered. Closing the doors, then the windows, she stared outside and gasped.

There! A white flash between trees. As it vanished, her heart hammered, making the pulse at her neck throb.

"Probably a stray dog," she murmured. Or all the brandy. "Yes, it's just my imagination." Shaking off the uneasy feeling by reminding herself that she'd felt jumpy since the funeral, she glanced at the pile of J.D.'s fan mail and the sympathy cards that had flooded the post office. Some of the letters had been written before J.D. died, and she wasn't surprised that so many woman claimed to be in love with him. Some offered to leave their husbands, or included risque pictures.

She lifted a sympathy card, addressed to her.

Dear Susannah,

If it wasn't for your husband's music, I never could have forgiven my man for his two-timing last year. But your husband's new record, *Songs for Susannah*, is so touching. And I knew my husband loved me the way your husband loved you. Now, ever since I let my man come back home, wearing that hangdog expression, he's stayed as straight as an arrow. Your man sang like an angel, and so many of his songs were about getting a second chance. Because of that, he helped a lot of people, and I just wanted you to know how he saved our marriage. He will be missed by the whole world.

Susannah wasn't going to get another chance. An unexpected tear splashed down her cheek. "Is this any way to get in the mood for Joe?" she muttered. She had to quit reading these letters and let go of the past.

The second most-sexy man she'd ever met had plans for her...all of which included sex. She needed to forget self-recriminations, as well as past anger that could never be resolved. "For once, enjoy yourself," she said. It had been a long time since she'd let herself feel good.

"I'll take a long bath, then make the bed with the silk sheets. I'll slip into a negligee, too," she decided. "Then hunt down candles and oils."

Joe had been wanting her for months, and two weeks ago she'd known it was high time she slept with him. Now, she tried to tell herself, nothing had changed. J.D. was gone, but her sex life wasn't over.

Knowing Joe, he'd make that plane, too. Which left her just enough time to spruce up. By the time he let himself in with his key, she'd be in bed waiting.

4

"WHAT SAY WE MAKE some magic, oh, Susannah?" J.D. whispered. "Maybe a little of our own bayou voodoo?" It was too dark to see him, but in the dream, his voice came from the foot of the bed as he curled his big hands around her feet. Playing musical instruments had strengthened his fingers, and the pads of his thumbs massaged deeply, rubbing dazzling circles. Long fingers dipped between each toe, stroking sensitive skin. Susannah tilted her chin up, her head, into the freshly laundered silk pillows.

Lifting both hands, she gripped the headboard of the brass bed where she and J.D. had made love so many times, then released a heartfelt sigh. "That feels good," she moaned.

Yes, only J.D.'s touch possessed the uncanny ability to always transport her to faraway places. With just a flick of a finger, he'd made the night vanish—the hooting owls and rustling leaves, and the gurgling creek and tree branches that traced the windowpanes.

The incredible feelings of her beloved touching her, made her crazy for his kisses. Nothing mattered, not when he was shifting his huge, warm, hands to the tops of her ankles, then casually kneading his way upward, palming her calves, smoothing her bare skin, penetrating the muscles.

"Concentrate very hard on what I'm doing, Susannah."

His voice—a slow, sugary drawl that had thrilled millions of women around the world—lowered, becoming barely audible, his tone teasingly seductive. "Are you concentrating?"

Was she awake or sleeping? Did it matter? Jitters of excitement leaped in her belly, feeling like drunken fireflies taking flight; their brilliant wings swept around her, making everything light up. Her senses sharpened and she felt a hitch inside her chest, then weightlessness since she couldn't quite catch her breath. Her nipples peaked, straining, and a bolt of heat as shattering as lightning shot to her lower belly and exploded. A moment passed, then the fire fizzled, curling up like a purring cat in front of a hearth. "I'm trying to concentrate," she managed throatily, "but you make it hard."

"I *am* hard."

Her heart stuttered, missing a beat, since she was imagining the thick bulge pressing against the fly of his jeans; she'd witnessed her husband's growing arousal thousands of times, but every time, she remained amazed by how fast he got turned on. "Well, that's not my doing," she said.

"I'm not so sure about that."

His voice was as sexy as the ministrations of his fingers— all dripping molasses and swirling sugar canes—and she yearned to hear it, right next to her ear. Maybe he'd play songs for her later and sing her to sleep, the way he had so many times before, or maybe he'd murmur sweet nothings until she shivered and she melted like ice on a hot day.

She wanted to feel his mouth ghosting across her lips, her neck, her cheeks. Then she wanted to experience what she'd been so sure she never would again—the cooler dampness of his tongue. She was imagining everything she wanted to feel…the tickle of his soft hair on her face, the burn of his whiskers on her belly, with the tiny, suckling love-bites he would pepper across her breasts. Yes…in a moment, he'd be a stallion champing the bit. Need would take the reins and pent-up passion would be unharnessed so it could run wild.

Moaning, she squeezed her eyes shut. All was sensation because he knew exactly how to touch her. Where and for how long. He liked to take his time, torturing her with enticing circular movements of strong hands.

Now the stress of the past months was slipping away. Like smoke caught in a strong wind, it stirred higher, whirling skyward, then it tumbled into clouds, vanishing. Could this be real, or was she crazy? Had Mama Ambrosia really foreseen this visitation, or had the strength of Susannah's memories conjured him…?

Yes, the strength of her love had burst through her anger, allowing them to share a final moment….

He had to be an angel. His touch was heavenly. Otherworldly. Ethereal. Surreal. Her mind went blank, hazing as he continued unlocking months of tension that had knotted up inside her. Yes…he was setting her free to love again, setting them both free.

Could they recapture passion, though? Could life return to the way it was before? She swallowed hard around a lump forming in her throat, fighting the urge to cry. Maybe. Oh, she hoped so!

She couldn't live without the old J.D., could she? Hadn't she told Ellie that? Hadn't she tried—and failed—in New York? And how could Ellie live without Robby, too? Life seemed so unfair! Fate would never force Susannah and her best friend to live without love that was meant to be!

Only J.D. knew how to negotiate the tangled maze of her forbidden zones, how to drive his hands deep down into the luscious corridors of her body, around the intricate map of her flesh, just as he was doing now. Only he knew how to correctly interpret her signs and signals. No one else knew that toying with her feet made her wild. Or that massaging the back of her neck could actually make her come. Or that lightly trailing fingers over her breasts could push her to the brink, but never take her all the way, only make her hover, at least until he kissed her.

"Yes," she whispered simply. He was tracing her inner thighs now, and she moaned, her hips arching, begging. He kept his nails trimmed, but long enough to pick guitar strings, and soon, he would rake those nails through her hair, the way he always did, when he wanted to make her super-hot. Licking her lips as she anticipated how he'd soon make her explode with lust, she was reminded that she, too, possessed keys to unlock his secret hot zones.

She opened her eyes, desperate to drink in his body, but could see nothing. She recalled every inch, though, like the back of her own hand. She knew his taut nipples, tender earlobes and inner thighs, then even more intimate places— the smooth skin rimming the head of his penis, the sensitive underside, the taut, steely ridge. Even without seeing, she knew he was hard and dusky with promise. She moaned once more, the sound a shudder, as his thumbs pressured the muscles of her calves deeply.

"Wider," he demanded parting her legs, speaking so softly she could barely hear him. "Open up, Susannah. Let me see everything."

A rustle sounded—he was leaning toward her now—then she felt the heated spear of his tongue. It trailed warm, wet loops upward, from her knees toward the apex of her thighs. Another onslaught of heat blanketed her, wrapping her in steamy bliss, and her hips lifted, urging his mouth toward where she most wanted it. His breath teased her core. Gently his tongue lapped the space above her pubic curls, dampening her silk panties until she shuddered with longing. "You won't see me tonight. Just feel me…feel everything, Susannah."

She parted her legs, further and as she did so, her nightie rose. She couldn't help but wish the light was on, since the delicate thong she wore would drive J.D. to distraction. But then, the darkness was freeing and seductive. Pitch-black, it formed a comforting cocoon in which she could play the brazen temptress, or coy girl, or scorned wife. It created the palette upon which they could paint their wildest, hottest, most wicked fantasies….

She couldn't see J.D., but she could imagine him, as surely as if the bedroom were bathed in light. Arousal had turned his blue eyes violet, the way it did sometimes, so they were the color of the sky in the darkest hours before the dawn. Usually sparkling with good humor, those eyes had gained a predatory glint, as if to say foreplay, however mild, had already reached the point of no return.

She sensed his broad shoulders were breaking a sweat, making his golden tan glisten and the sprawling crop of black hair on his chest gleam. Her eyes followed the trail of curls, and she studied where it tapered between pectorals, then raced down his flat tummy. Resting his hands on her knees, his fingers tightened, and she heard a pant of breath. "Oh, Susannah," he sang. "Now don't you cry for me…"

And then the room was silent again. So silent, that she could have been alone after all. Suddenly she wished she'd put on another CD. "Are you there?" she whispered.

He was there all right. His tongue, anyway. Slow, torturous pinwheels teased one thigh, then the other. Then he crooked one of her legs, lifting it higher, his kisses deepening until he was suckling hard, drawing skin between his lips, surely leaving marks, and she plunged, spiraling downward into oblivion.

Just as whiskers roughened her skin, his tongue soothed, then love bites wounded her once more. Everything seemed to be underwater, as if they were making love on the bottom of a pool. Silk was swimming over silk, and she had no idea where his saliva ended and her juices began.

Dangerously, she arched, insisting on feeling more of his mouth, and as he delivered, her heart swelled. Fate had returned him to her. Maybe this was their last chance. Releasing her grip on the headboard, she brought her hands to the mattress and rested them at her sides, ready to grab his shoulders, wanting to drag him on top of her, but also wanting to draw out the pleasure.

He seemed to vanish once more, and she gasped, wondering where he'd gone, but then a fingernail traced her panties. A whine tore from her throat.

His mouth disappeared. Then she heard him shrug off one of the shirts he so rarely bothered to wear. A swoosh followed as he stepped from boots and socks. Brass clanked—his belt buckle. Then a snap popped, followed by the sound of metallic teeth as he slowly dragged down a zipper.

"Take them off," she whispered.

His scarcely audible chuckle hung in the silence, then from somewhere outside, cicadas whirred and an owl hooted. He climbed onto the bed, his knee landing between her legs, his weight depressing the mattress. Hairy legs, not denim, brushed her inner thighs. She shivered in anticipation, tracing a hand over his bare back.

She was waking up, realizing it wasn't a dream. "Now we're getting somewhere," she whispered. Vaguely, from somewhere far off, she thought she heard something…a phone ringing? A dead bolt turning? A door opening?

And then, for a second, everything seemed jumbled. Had she drifted back to sleep? Was the downstairs mantle clock chiming the hour? Was it midnight? But no…hadn't it just been two in the morning? How long ago?

She'd tumbled into some netherworld, a fantasy land between waking and sleeping, where rationality ceased. Here, in the darkness of dreams, nothing bad had come between her and J.D., and emotion surged, making her heart feel full to bursting. All at once, she felt as overwhelmed with joy as she had on her wedding day.

Was she going to treat him like a ghost in his own house forever? And how could she have felt so possessive about Banner Manor, anyway? When she thought of her selfishness, tears stung her eyes. She felt J.D. brush his lips against the strands of her hair. "My home is wherever you are, sweetheart. It could be a shack in a swamp, for all I care."

"Love me," she sighed.

I always have, Susannah, and I always will.

Had he really said the words, or had she only thought them? "Now."

Not tomorrow?

"I needed you yesterday."

A burning finger fluttered over her panties again; this time, he parted her folds through the silk. Softly grunting with pure male hunger, he seemingly registered how ready she was, right before his mouth settled on hers for a claiming kiss.

Against her belly, she felt his hand curl over the waistband, and he ripped down the silk, slowly dragging it over the lengths of her legs. Heat flushed her face. She was drenched and aching, her breasts chaffing the negligee. Instead of feeling nice and soft, it felt rougher now and much more bothersome. She had to get rid of it! Gripping the hem, she pulled the nightie over her head, tossing it away just as his fingers threaded into her pubic curls, toying. When he tugged lightly, she disintegrated, into bundles of knotted nerves, and her hips twisted from the mattress, moving involuntarily, urging him on.

"I missed this," she whispered.

What? Making love?

He hadn't actually spoken, had he?

Her hands cupped the bunched muscles of his shoulders, pulling him close. Gliding upward, he lay on top of her, skin to skin. His rigid flesh was burning, pressed where she was hot, moist and open, and she felt as skittish as a colt. He delivered a series of butterfly kisses.

"Never leave me again," she murmured, her lips barely moving.

She heard his voice in her mind. *You left me.*

But she hadn't…not really. Not in her heart. How could he have hurt her so much? *Only because you made me.*

I'd never make you do anything, Susannah.

Liar. He was supposed to be her one true love, her whole life, her family. Sliding a hand between them, he reached between her legs, cupping her pubis, and she rocked against his damp palm, melting and gasping when he squeezed. In response, he pressed the heel of his hand harder, and his mouth found hers, his firm lips nuzzling hers apart. His tongue followed. Hers met it with fire as it moved, languid and thick, pushing deeper, testing her teeth, exploring her inner cheeks. Lower, the love-slick tip of a finger circled her clitoris, gathering moisture as his tongue began thrusting.

"Oh…oh," she whispered against his lips as two thick fingers entered her. Her hips slammed upward, her backside tightening as her nails dug into his shoulders, encouraging each maddening touch. His free hand tilted her chin farther back, and he changed the angle of his mouth on hers, slanting across her lips one way, then another, while he loved her with his fingers, strumming her until need consumed her....

In this netherworld, their love was protected and no harm could come to it, she thought. There was only hopeless desperation filling her as she climbed, nothing more. She was drowning in his kisses, lost. A surge of heat swept her away, and she felt desperate to come—she had to come!—

"Please," she begged, reeling as his fingers quickened. "You're good...so good..." There was no other man for her. No other who could solicit such explosive responses.

His mouth crushed down on hers and his free hand found a breast. Squeezing and pinching the nipple, he made her scream with pleasure. The night seemed so strange and dark and silent. Starless and moonless. Curtains of foliage beyond the windows further blocked any light, and the rain had ceased. She could see nothing at all....

Only feel.

He dragged his mouth from to her chin, then to her breasts. Ragged and labored, his breaths came in hoarse, raspy tufts as he twisted his magical fingers inside her. *Sleight of hand.* Her belly somersaulted as his tongue simultaneously swirled a nipple, licking circles, but not lingering, trailing farther down to her solar plexus...and down to her ribs...and down to her navel....

Heat exploded in her tummy. Yearning claimed her. Fever took her, her whole body boiling. Chest hair brushed her thighs. She gasped as his mouth dropped. His fingers were still inside her, but he was catching her curls between his teeth now, too. And suddenly, he burrowed, nuzzling his face, muttering senseless nothings.

She whimpered mindlessly as his tongue parted her, cold

where she was burning. The whole pad of his tongue sponged her, and she bucked, threading fingers into his hair. Thick and wavy, they rushed over her hands. Fisting the strands, she dragged his mouth closer, until his tongue went wild, the side of it laving her clitoris. Like a flame guttering in a dark, windy room, the tip flicked the bud.

Her quivering thighs wrapped around his neck. Spurred on, he hugged her close and she rode him shamelessly, wild for the kisses, her knees bracketing his head. His scent, so strong and arousing and male, mixed with her musk. She wanted to touch him everywhere, to do everything with him....

But she was powerless; he was feasting as if he'd never taste her again. As she shattered, her cry rent the silence of the room and her hands grasped blindly. Once more, she clawed at the air. He was gone!

But no! She'd lost control, the orgasm was so strong. A hard, hot, heavy chest was sliding upward now, before she could catch her breath, crushing down on her, his rock-hard muscles a salve for her aching breasts. Her insides were mush, but she realized he was only getting started when he uttered a strangled sigh and roughly, without apology, used his knee to push hers aside, creating access.

He covered her mouth once more, his lips possessive. The taste was tinged with her flavor, and when he thrust his tongue, tears of joy mixed with the kiss, and she reached between them, her fingers hungrily wrapping around his familiar length, fisting him, urging him inside. Relief seemed to fill him as a stroke parted her, and tension left his shoulders as the sensation burned away the last veil of civility.

They'd crashed through another dimension. Reality was a dream now. And dreams, the reality. As he filled her, his body straining, desire overwhelmed her once more. Her hands busily remembered each nip and tuck as they roved around the column of his neck, then the sharp bones between his shoulders. She traced the ridge of his spine and the curves of his taut backside, and she climbed once more, flying toward more pleasure.

Any second could be their last, she thought vaguely, her mind clouded by desire. She'd lost J.D. once. Now she had to be careful. She could never let him go. As she came again, she felt his body tighten into a wall of hard rocks and ridges—then he gushed. Although she could never bring this man close enough, she tried, gripping him like a vise. Her arms felt like ropes circling him a hundred times, and silently, she vowed that she'd never let go.

Holding him, she listened to his breathing become even. Slowly, as sleep overtook her, her hands relaxed. Probably, against her will, she dozed….

"What?" she suddenly muttered, batting her eyes, blinking against the darkness, trying to get her bearings. She remembered hugging J.D., and telling herself not to let go, but then she had. He was no longer on top of her, but it was still night. Wishing there was a clock in the room, she whispered, "J.D.?"

Her heart suddenly stuttered, her mind racing. "Oh no…" Her hand flew to her mouth, covering it. She'd been dreaming….

Yes…Joe must have entered the house after she'd fallen asleep and used the key Ellie had given him

"Joe?" she managed.

She could swear she'd just seen a shadow at the door. Had he been standing there? Had he realized she'd been lost in a fantasy? Quickly, she reached across the bed, but it was empty. Tears stung her eyes. Her love for J.D. hadn't conjured his spirit, after all. He was really gone. Forever.

"Joe?"

No answer. Her mind must have latched onto Mama Ambrosia's ridiculous claims. Well...in the cold light of day, it would take more than a little brandy to make her forgive J.D. He'd tortured her with his shenanigans while alive, and apparently, he was going to continue to do so by haunting her dreams.

Realizing she really was naked, she slipped a hand down and checked. Obviously the lovemaking hadn't been the work of a phantom.

Maybe Joe hadn't heard her say J.D.'s name. Maybe he'd just gone downstairs or to the bathroom. She felt the heat of a blush warm her cheeks in the darkness. He might not be J.D., but the lovemaking had been amazing.

She groaned, her head pounding when she started to get up. "Forget it," she murmured sleepily. No doubt, he'd come back to bed soon.

And she'd be right here waiting.

5

"WHAT HAPPENED LAST NIGHT?" Susannah croaked, vaguely wondering what was pulling her from sleep. Oh! J.D. had been here....

But no, everything was coming back. "Joe?" Her mind racing, she squinted, needles of sunlight piercing her eyes, then she glanced beside her. "Not a man in sight," she whispered.

She tingled all over. Transported, she could feel the lap of her lover's tongue, the depth of his kisses, the grip of his hug. For a moment, all was darkness. She and her lover's bodies were joined again, damp with perspiration and completely inseparable. They were riding into oblivion under the canopy of a full moon and bright stars. She needed more....

Shivers danced down her back. Then more recollections intruded, and she gasped. Had Joe gotten mad? Had he realized she'd fantasized he was J.D.? Yes, that's what she'd been thinking as she'd fallen asleep, wasn't it? Had he left last night?

She hoped not. Remembering Joe's hot, husky whispers, a delicious chill swept over her. And to think she'd believed making love to Joe wouldn't be good. Ellie was right—Joe's voice, body type and hair were enough like J.D.'s that Susannah must have suspended disbelief.

Finally Susannah had slept with a man other than J.D.

Johnson. Definitely a red-letter day. As a surge of hope and renewed possibility sang inside her, she realized a phone was ringing, the sound muffled. Rummaging through a mound of J. D.'s clothes, which she'd been sorting the other day. "Hello?"

No answer.

"Who's calling please?" Straining, she heard breathing. Something, she wasn't sure what, made her believe the caller was a woman.

"Who is this?" she demanded more insistently.

A click sounded, then there was the dial tone. Swallowing hard, she recalled the hang-up call she'd received the night the *Alabama* had exploded. The second she put down the phone, it rang again. This time, she answered sharply. "Who's there?"

"Are you okay?"

Relief flooded her. "Joe!"

He sounded concerned. "Who did you think it was?"

"I got a crank call just now," she explained in a rush, her lips broadening into a smile. Ten to one he'd found her car keys and run into town, letting her sleep. "Where did you go?"

"Uh…that's why I called. I wanted to apologize for last night."

Was he crazy? "What for?"

"For pushing you to get more involved."

"No, that's okay," she murmured, wishing she'd given in sooner. "I needed a good kick in the butt. Otherwise I couldn't have made the leap." Her gaze settling on the window, she realized it was later than she'd thought, maybe noon, and she stretched once more.

"Did you go to the store or something?" she asked, coming more fully awake. "Did you take my keys or rent a car when you got in? If you're near the main drag, there's a place called

Delia's Diner. I'd love some of her strawberry-rhubarb pie."
Thank goodness! It seemed that Joe hadn't guessed she'd
been dreaming about J.D. or he would have said something.

"Uh…I'm not in town, Susannah. That's what I wanted to
talk to you about."

So he *had* realized she'd been fantasizing about J.D.! Her
mental gears did a three-sixty. "Oh, Joe, I'm so sorry…."

"Don't be. It's my fault. Last night, after we spoke, I
realized you're not ready. I never should have pursued you."

"How could you say that after last night?"

"Because, like I said, I could hear your real feelings. You'll
be ready for somebody else someday, but not now. I know
you're grieving." Pausing, he exhaled a soft curse. "And I can't
take advantage of that. If you want the truth, someday I hope
I find half of what you two had. J.D. was your life, and I had
no right to involve myself. You weren't even divorced. Last
night I knew we shouldn't keep trying. Fate wasn't on our
side, Susannah. It was just bad timing."

Her head was starting to spin again. Nothing he said made
sense. "You still feel that way? Even after last night?"

"I know you were sincere on the phone, that you wanted
me to come, but…"

A female giggle interrupted. "Joe, the shower's ready!"

Susannah recognized her voice. Tara Jones. "Uh…where
are you?"

"Chicago. That's what I've been trying to tell you. Oh
God, Susannah, I'm sorry. Tara asked me to help her, and one
thing led to another, and we wound up—"

In bed. Susannah's heart hammered. "This can't be happening," she whispered.

"I didn't think you'd take it so hard. To be honest, I figured
you'd be relieved."

Had he really not been here last night? And if not, who had been in her bed? "You weren't here?"

"No." Now he sounded confused. "Why would you think so?"

"Because…" She swallowed hard. She'd shared a bed with someone, and if it wasn't Joe— Abruptly, and without explanation, she ended the call and dialed star-six-nine. The phone was answered on the first ring.

"Hilton Hotel, Chicago."

Breath whooshed from her lungs. Her pulse started pounding so hard that her heart seemed to be beating in her throat. She tried to push questions from her mind, desperate not to ponder the impossible. The ghost of J. D. Johnson couldn't have made love to her. She could barely find her voice. "Joe O'Grady's room please."

"I'll connect you."

He answered on the second ring. "Susannah?"

"It's me," she said, hearing faint rustling on the other end of the line, which meant Tara was still in there. "Uh…I think we were disconnected."

"Aren't we past that, Susannah?" he asked. "Haven't we been as honest as possible? Let's not stop now. I know you hung up on me, but like I said, I didn't think you'd take this so hard."

"I didn't hang up because I was angry," she argued. "Oh, never mind," she added, knowing he wouldn't believe her. "I'm fine. Really. I'm happy for you. It's just that…"

"What?"

Her lips parted, but what could she say? That she had reason to believe they'd shared a night of passion? That those reasons were still evident—in the purplish bruises left by some man's possessive mouth on her thighs, and the burn left by his whiskers. She'd awakened feeling guilty, for pretending Joe was J.D., but now… "You really weren't here?"

she whispered, needing to clarify it once more, panic over-whelming her.

"What did you say? Sorry, but you're mumbling."

"Nothing," she managed. "I didn't say anything impor-tant." In fact, she could think of absolutely nothing to say now, so she simply added, "Thanks for calling, Joe."

"I'll call Ellie and have her ask June to come so June can come to Banner Manor," he said. "I'm worried about you."

"Don't call June." If Susannah couldn't explain last night to Joe, she wouldn't be able to explain it to her sister, either. "Uh…in fact," she lied, "I was just headed over to her house. I was just about to go out the door when you called."

"Good." His voice softened. "No hard feelings?"

"None."

"Can we see each other when you come for the awards ceremony tomorrow? We're flying back today."

"I'll try."

"And if, uh…"

"If you're with Tara when she sings, it won't be awkward," she assured him, still wondering who had been in her bed. Even now, she could feel his magical fingers so like J.D.'s, touching her. Still, her lover couldn't have been a ghost. His touch had been too real, as visceral as anything she'd ever felt.

"You're great," Joe was saying. "So understanding."

She barely heard him. As she hung up, her mind was doing cartwheels. She gasped. What if the man been some member of J.D.'s entourage? How many men had keys to the house?

"It was J.D.," she whispered. "I know it."

But how could that be? The man had smelled like him, felt like him, touched her in all the familiar ways. Her throat con-stricting with worry, she glanced once more at the marks on her thighs. Oh yes, they were real enough, just as real as the love bites on her shoulders. Real, too, was the craving she still felt this morning. She wanted to feel the viselike grip of his arms encircling her again, the hard, muscular heat of his wall-like body pressing insistently against hers. Warmth flushed through her, and she was aware of her melting feminine core.

Rising and pulling the sheet with her, she headed toward the bathroom, then stopped in her tracks. "What?" she murmured, wishing her renegade heart wasn't beating so dangerously out of control.

After the funeral, Susannah had hung J.D.'s favorite hat, the red-and-black hunting cap with the oversize ear flaps, over the bedpost, but now, it was snagged on the neck of a guitar in the corner of the room. "Exactly where he used to leave it," she managed to whisper.

Worse, in the shoe rack hanging on the open closet door, all her shoes had been switched so the rights and lefts were in the wrong slots.

That, too, was a sign J. D. Johnson had come calling.

"ANSWER YOUR PHONE," Susannah whispered twenty minutes later. She knew better than to drive while using her cell, but her circumstances required desperate measures. She'd thrown on the first outfit she'd found—one of J.D.'s favorite dresses, a strapless yellow number printed with blue flowers—and now she was speeding toward Mama Ambrosia's.

"Please," she whispered as she passed Delia's Diner, her free hand gripping the wheel so tightly that her knuckles turned bright pink, then white. "Dammit." Sweat beaded on her forehead as she spun the dial on the AC. The bayou heat was particularly unbearable today. Leaves from the towering moss-covered oaks created a canopy over an otherwise shimmering roadway, but none of the shade was helping. She just hoped she could find the fortune-teller's cabin. It was tucked in the woods and reputedly difficult to locate.

"Robriquet here."

Finally. "Robby?"

"Susannah." He sounded surprised, maybe even hopeful, and now she felt bad. Probably, he thought she was calling with news about Ellie. "What's up?"

She could hear the sounds of Lee Polls—the whir of fax and copy machines and shrill ring of phones were as familiar to her as J.D.'s reflection in a mirror, because she'd called to talk to Ellie so many times. Now she pictured Ellie's ex-lover sitting at the desk that should have been Ellie's, his lanky, muscular body sprawled in a chair. She hesitated, then cut to the chase. "Robby, I think I saw J.D."

During the long, ensuing pause, she inadvertently tapped her foot on the gas pedal, making the car lurch. "Robby? Are you still there?"

"Uh…yeah. What do you mean you *saw* J.D.?"

"I know it sounds crazy, but last night he was in our house. I mean, I didn't actually see him," she amended. "It was too dark."

His tone was dubious. "Where are you?"

"In the car, on my way to Mama Ambrosia's. You're not going to believe this, but she's been calling, saying I should expect a visitation from J.D.—"

"Whoa," Robby said, concern in his voice. "I don't want you going over there, filling your head with that crazy lady's mumbo-jumbo." He lowered his voice. "J.D.'s gone, Susannah, and she's trying to take advantage of your vulnerability for a few dollars. I don't want to see you get hurt any more than you already have been. I'm saying this as your friend and J.D.'s. He'd want me to look after you. Come to Lee Polls and we'll call June. She told me you haven't been picking up the phone, and after work, I intended to come to Banner Manor and check on you, but it looks like I might have to pull an all-nighter. Ever since Ellie left, things have been a mess around here."

"I'm fine," Susannah protested.

"We're worried about you. You're not acting like yourself. June says you're still playing J.D.'s records twenty-four-seven and wearing his old shirts. You're wandering around the house in a daze, and now you're saying he was actually *in* the house. What do you mean? Did you see him?"

"No, not really. I told you it was dark."

"You either did or you didn't."

She wasn't about to offer the details of what happened, at least not to Robby. Just thinking about the encounter made heat flood her body once more, and this time it sure had nothing to do with the sweltering bayou. Her eyes stung, burning with unshed tears. "I'm not crazy. He was my husband, Robby."

"I know that, honey. But he's gone. Sometimes people get real distraught in grief, the way you are now, and—"

"I'm not lying," she managed, as she pulled off the main road onto a narrow one lane byway. She scanned the road for signs of the cabin. Hunching over the wheel, she wondered if she was going in the right direction, not that she'd ask Robby. "Something strange happened last night. That's all I know."

"Strange how?"

She thought of the smooth, huge hands massaging her feet, exploring her ankles and gliding all the way up her body. "Just strange. And this morning, I got a hang-up call. I thought it might be J.D."

"It couldn't have been."

"Next thing you know, you'll be saying I'm as fanciful as my mama. But I'm not. Last night—"

"Your mama *was* delicate, Susannah," Robby interjected. "You're a lot more grounded, true, but you're more like her than you want to admit. It's nothing to be ashamed of. You've been under so much stress—"

"Don't patronize me," she warned.

"I'm not. I just—"

"Oh, forget it," she muttered, angry at herself for expecting support when she couldn't figure out if it was real, either. "June will say exactly the same thing. Ellie, too. You'll all think I'm crazy, and maybe I am."

"That's not what I meant."

"No, you're right," she forced herself to say, hoping she sounded more reasonable.

"What did you actually see?"

"Nothing. That's just it. I think I just had a dream."

Squinting against the sun dappling the hood of the car, she finally saw her destination wink through the trees, an abysmal little log cabin with a sagging wraparound porch and bright pink curtains. She turned down a red dirt trail, overgrown with weeds, and inched the car forward. "Robby, I'm glad I called. What would I do without you? You're so reasonable. The dream I had just seemed so real."

"Do me a favor," Robby said as she pulled beneath an out-cropping of trees and behind an old, wheel-less car perched on cinder-blocks. "Just don't go to Mama Ambrosia's."

"Okay," she said. But what other choice did she have? she wondered, staring at the fortune teller's house.

"I mean it," Robby continued. "I know J.D. always let her read his cards and look into her crystal ball, but I think you should go to your sister's house instead. Promise me?"

"Scout's honor," Susannah lied as she eyed the front door. No light seemed to be on inside. "I'd better not keep talking while I'm driving."

"Well, don't get mad at me for saying you can be a little like your mama."

"When?" she couldn't help but ask.

"You were always thinking J.D. was having affairs."

She thought of Sandy Smithers. "He did."

"Never happened."

"Whatever, Robby," she muttered.

"Now, don't let your mind run wild."

Susannah sighed. "I'll drive over to June's right now."

"Great. I'll try to check on you later tonight."

Susannah tried to shake off another bout of sadness, but she couldn't. Robby was a decent man, just as J.D. had been, so it was no wonder Ellie had once cared for him. He'd gotten fed up with J.D.'s antics, but seemed to have forgiven him now that he'd passed. "I'll be fine," she said contritely before hanging up.

Then she got out of the car. As she did, a black cat darted from the front porch and into the underbrush. Not a good sign. Nor was how deafening the car door sounded in the silence when she closed it. Leaves rustled in the surrounding woods, and suddenly, as she headed down the walkway, everything felt strangely desolate.

Although the day was sunny and the mercury was shooting into the stratosphere, a shudder meandered down her spine, moving as slow as a gator in a swamp, worrying each vertebrae. "At least Mama Ambrosia will believe me," she muttered, just to hear her own voice.

When she reached the front door, a weathered wooden affair, she noticed a message board hanging over the doorknob. Written on it, in capital letters, were the words: *On Vacation*.

Her lips parted in astonishment. "On vacation?"

"Well, I was just about to go," a voice boomed behind her.

She whirled. "Mama Ambrosia!" The woman was only a few paces away. Startled, Susannah brought her hand up to her chest. "How did you creep up on me like that?"

"I have my ways."

The woman looked as mysterious as she always did. Brightly colored rags were twirled in her braided hair and a huge tent of a housedress covered her bulky frame. Beaded sandals adorned her feet, and she wore countless ankle bracelets.

She came forward, her steps heavy, her great weight shifting from side to side, and she squinted against the sun. "Why, I can't believe how you just yelled out my name, as if you were surprised to see me! Who were you expecting?"

"Nobody. I just—"

"Nobody? Now, how could nobody be here? And why would you visit nobody? Only a somebody can be in a house, missy."

She wanted to know the identity of the man in her house the previous night. Was he a somebody? A nobody? Whatever the case, Mama Ambrosia's manner was already making Susannah a little testy. "You're not really in a house," she said, since the woman was always so contrary. "You're outside."

"I won't be if I go in."

Finding the woman impossible, Susannah said, "Look, I just wanted to talk to you for a minute."

"I warn you, if you want advice, I'm on vacation." As if expecting an argument, she continued. "Everybody has to go on vacation. Even fortune-tellers."

"I never said otherwise," Susannah agreed. "But, well...I hope you won't leave just yet. I need to ask you about our conversation on the phone last night."

Mama Ambrosia shot her an innocent glance. "Did we speak?"

Since the woman had called a number of times, Susannah found the comment completely exasperating, but she forced herself to stay calm. For whatever reason, Mama Ambrosia strived to be difficult, but there wasn't much Susannah could do about that. "You said J.D. would visit me."

"Was I right or was I right?"

Little choice there, Susannah thought, so she said, "I think you were right."

"Well, glory be," murmured Mama Ambrosia.

"Can you tell me anything more?" Susannah asked in a rush, now that she'd gotten the woman's attention.

Mama Ambrosia glanced behind her, toward a clearing, and Susannah noticed a late-model SUV with luggage strapped to the rack.

"I don't want to hold you up," she assured her. "It'll only take a moment. Where is J.D.? Is he all right? Is he…" Susannah didn't know how to ask. "A ghost? Can he come back?"

Mama Ambrosia nodded gravely. "This is an emergency."

Without another word, she reached into a pocket, withdrew a key, stepped past Susannah and unlocked the door. Susannah followed. The interior was dim, lit only by whatever sunlight pierced the curtains, and it was pungent with scents of incense, herbs and spices that lined shelves in the front room.

Mama indicated a table near a window. "Sit."

As Susannah took a seat, goose bumps rose on her arms. "It was so real," she found herself saying. "He was in our room…"

Mama Ambrosia chuckled softly as she seated herself opposite Susannah, placed a black velvet swatch on the table, then a transparent ball on top of that. "In your room?"

"Yes."

Placing her hands on the globe, Mama peered into its depths.

"You don't take the ball with you?" Susannah asked, mostly out of sheer nervousness.

"On vacation?" Mama Ambrosia shook her head in consternation. "Clients," she grumbled. "They never allow you a moment's rest. Ask me, your husband had the right idea."

"Right idea?" Susannah echoed.

"In shuffling off the mortal coil."

Once more, Mama Ambrosia seemed to be speaking gibberish. "Do you see anything?"

"Not yet," Mama returned testily. "This isn't like a TV, missy. You can't just turn it on."

Susannah winced. "Sorry."

Long moments passed. "You're not a believer, are you?" Mama suddenly said.

Susannah wasn't sure. "In what?"

"Magic."

She started to say no, but then she heard J.D.'s liquid-velvet voice sound in her ear, as surely as if he were in the room. "Want to play scarves and cards, Susannah? Hats and rabbits?" His slow drawl moved like the bayou's tributaries, lazily winding around her until her knees melted. "Some magic."

"Which kind?"

She could barely find her voice. "J.D.'s and my magic, I guess. I mean, I never believed in the supernatural. I believe in God, of course, but beyond that, I believe in…in human magic I guess." Emotion made her voice husky. "Love." She paused. "That's magic, isn't it?"

"The best kind, child." The woman's hands were floating above the ball now. "You say he came to you…how?"

A blush made her cheeks burn. It was none of the woman's

business, but she might be the only person who she could help. "He made love to me."

"Hmm. He seems very real. Very close. As if he's not a ghost at all."

Susannah's heart leaped. "Will I see him again?"

"Soon."

"When?"

Mama Ambrosia shook her head. "Maybe tonight. Or tomorrow. I see…a golden key in your future. I see an auditorium filled with people. The men are wearing tuxedos, and the women are dressed in beautiful gowns."

"The awards ceremony!" Susannah exclaimed. Apparently Mama Ambrosia really did see the future. "I'm going to New York tomorrow morning. J.D. was nominated for an award, and if he wins, I'm accepting it for him."

The woman's inky eyebrows knitted with concentration, then she abruptly lifted her hand from the ball.

"What?" Susannah asked.

"Nothing."

"What did you see? Something bad?"

"Nothing, child."

Susannah grasped her arm, and was surprised by the muscular firmness. Mama Ambrosia was a heavy woman, but strong, too. "You have to tell me." Why was the woman hedging? Just a moment ago, she'd been more forthcoming. What was wrong?

"There is danger in your future," the woman whispered.

Susannah's heart thudded hard against her ribs. "What do you mean?"

"I don't know. That's all I see."

"Danger from J.D.?"

"No. He will save you."

"From what? How?"

The woman shook her head. "Sometimes I see the future, but other times, the future is something my clients have to live." Standing, she said, "You have to go now."

Just like that? With even more uncertainty than before? Feeling stunned and not knowing what to believe, Susannah rose to her feet. "Thank you for what you were able to tell me."

"Don't worry, you'll be fine in the end."

In the end? Was Mama Ambrosia a charlatan, as many claimed, or did she really see the future? And if so, what danger lurked around the corner?

Whatever the case, a plan was forming in Susannah's mind. Tomorrow, she would fly to New York for the awards ceremony, but tonight, she would battle all her inner demons, and wait for whoever—or whatever—came calling. In truth, fear would be a small price to pay if she could re-experience the hot sex she'd had last night.

Yes. She'd stay awake. And if the ghost of her late husband appeared she would catch him.

6

FINGERS WERE TRAINING SLOWLY up her ribs with a teasing tickle, and Susannah sucked in a quick breath of anticipation as warm hands molded over her breasts, deeply massaging, making her melt. Finding both nipples, her mysterious lover toyed until they ached, playing with the stiffening tips until she offered a shuddering sigh.

"Miss me, Susannah?"

Sexual frustration was building inside her, and J.D.'s seductive drawl didn't help, since it acted on her like a drug. "No, I don't. Why, everybody knows I'm better off without you, J. D. Johnson. Any woman would be. Any man, too. In fact, you can add kids and pets to that list."

"But you love me, anyway?"

"Not anymore," she returned, but she snaked her arms around his neck and tugged him closer.

He felt so good and hard, a lean, rangy male with sculpted, taut thighs that fell between hers, not to mention knees that pressed insistently, wordlessly telling her what he wanted. Angling his head, he swiped his mouth sideways across hers. The friction wasn't much, just a delightful graze of warm, smooth lips, but the kiss burned.

"C'mon, say you still love me."

But she didn't. She never could again. It was over between

them. Against his mouth, she whispered, "Didn't I tell you never to darken our doorstep again?"

"Is that why your arms are wrapped around me?"

He would point out the discrepancy. He was breaking her resistance, and each time his lips brushed hers, she felt more languid and insubstantial; when he feathered butterfly kisses down the length of her neck, she felt as if she were floating, as if she might blow away like a flower in the wind. Twisting her head so his lips couldn't land on hers again, she muttered, "I hate you, J.D."

"I can tell."

She forced herself to let go of him, feeling strangely bereft as she did so, then she planted her hands on his shoulders and pushed. Not hard enough to make him back away, she realized, but at least she wasn't twining around him like a vine, which was what she most wanted to do. She was weak. At least when it came to him. She'd become attuned to him, learning the idiosyncrasies of his body as well as those of her own, committing them to memory, just so she could drive him crazy with lust….

Suddenly, she startled awake. Abruptly her eyes blinked open. She lay perfectly still, realizing that she'd been dreaming. Just as before, her sensual fantasies seemed impossibly real. Perspiration coated her skin. Her heart was racing, too. Her hand was still curled around a baseball bat that lay next to her, in case she needed protection. Beyond that, she'd stuffed pillows under the covers, to make it look as if she was sleeping.

She bit back a gasp. Yes, something had awakened her. Downstairs. Tightening her grip on the bat, she listened, barely able to hear over the blood rushing in her ears. What time was it? Was someone really in the house? How long had she slept?

So much for keeping guard. Clamping her upper teeth down

on her lower lip, she listened. Yes, she strained to hear. A door hinge, squeaking floorboards, soft steps. *Breathe in, breathe out,* she thought. *Stay calm. Don't alert him. If it is a him...*

She had to get out of bed. But would he hear her? Silently, she damned herself for lying down. But she'd waited so long, and she'd gotten tired. Too bad it was such a moonless, starless night. Whatever light might have illuminated the room was obscured by the curtains, and as her eyes adjusted, she could make out vague shapes, the outline of a dresser and night table, a lamp and chair. She wasn't about to turn on the bedside lamp, not yet. Leaving it off had been part of her plan.

Soundlessly she scooted back in bed, resting against the headboard before swinging her feet to the floor. She'd slept in a T-shirt and sweatpants. When her toes touched the floor, the boards creaked and she froze.

Someone was in the house and she was sure that he'd heard her. Her senses heightened, her muscles grew painfully rigid. Who—or what—was downstairs? A ghost? An intruder? A friend or family member with the key? Maybe her sister, June?

Stealthily, someone was creeping upstairs. She definitely heard steps now...slow, deliberate, cautious. Or was her mind playing tricks? She hoped so. That seemed better than most alternatives. Maybe the separation from J.D., then his death, had simply been too much for her.

Icy panic threaded through her veins. Any sensible woman would have gone to June's this morning, she thought. Or to Lee Polls. Or back to the New York apartment she shared with Ellie. Anywhere but here.

And yet how could Susannah leave this bedroom, when she could still smell the scent of the man's aroused, naked, sweating flesh and feel his heat as he crushed down on top of her, his passion as his tongue thrust against hers with senseless abandon? How, when her hands were still molding over his rock-hard muscles, squeezing what felt like sculpted bronze.

Was a phantom about to make love to her again?

Only the heat of last night could cause her to act as foolishly as she was now. Her craving was visceral, inarguable, complete. She'd do anything to feel that passion again....

The hands she'd felt were like a substance to which she'd become addicted—his touch on her bare skin, the only possible fix. Feeling him inside her, pushing deep, dragging her over the top with him was a pleasure she anticipated like a slow, enticing burn. He'd reignited a spark she'd believed gone forever, then left embers glowing, ready to flare into a torch of fire. She wanted to unbridle the lust, give it full rein, let it run wild. A thousand nights would never be enough....

Suddenly her eyes darted toward the window, seeking escape, but she was on the second floor, too far to jump, not that she would. She had to risk whatever was about to happen, to know the truth....

Something made a noise near the upstairs landing.

Get up, she thought. *Right now. Hurry. Don't make a sound.* Gritting her teeth, fearing he'd hear her, she shifted her weight, praying the mattress springs wouldn't creak as she rose, clutching the bat. Her hands were slick with sweat, and she felt she could lose her grip any second.

As soon as she was on her feet, she swayed, whoozy. She'd awakened too abruptly, stood too soon, and anxiety was flooding her body. Using the bat as a crutch, she steadied herself, the back of her throat going bone dry. There was definitely someone in the hallway. Could it be Robby? she wondered. He'd said he was going to check on her, and he'd always had a key. On impulse, she almost called his name, then thought the better of it. What if it wasn't him?

Besides, he'd knock, wouldn't he? She swung the bat to her shoulder. Was this the danger about which Mama Ambrosia had warned? If so, how could J.D. save her, as the woman had claimed?

She sensed someone near the doorway. Slowly, Susannah exhaled, her breath shallow. Would the intruder believe she was sleeping? Could that buy her time to see his face?

She crept soundlessly backward, melting further into shadows, then she inched her free hand to the bedside lamp, pinching the chain between a thumb and forefinger.

As soon as the person came near, she'd snap on the light, and then, if she didn't like what she saw, she was going to use the bat, no questions asked.

Then she'd run like hell.

A shadow filled the doorway. She almost gasped. Scents of pine and nuts, along with peppermints infused the air, and the second after that, the whole room seemed to fill with J.D.'s presence. Her reaction wasn't something she could qualify or quantify. As surely as she was standing there, though, he was here. In the room. With her.

She parted her lips to speak, but she was in too much shock to utter a sound. She tried not to breathe, but his scent was traveling across the room and into her lungs, anyway. She damned her body's traitorous response, knowing the prickles of awareness dancing through her system had less to do with fear than desire. Despite the strange circumstances, or perhaps because of them, breathless anticipation swept over her.

He'd brought the night with him…a thick darkness, a sense of mystery, a promise that hidden secrets would be revealed. Something impenetrable existed here, something she suspected the room's light could never pierce, should she turn it on. Suddenly, every molecule smelled and felt different, charged with unexpected electricity.

He seemed to be emitting sparks in the inky darkness, so they flew every which way, including in her direction. In reality, he was hazy, a mere outline as motionless as a statue. Judging from what she sensed was the tilt of his head, he hadn't yet realized she was awake and watching him....

She tried to stay silent as he started approaching the bed, the movement so fluid he could have been floating. He was still a mere shadow, a phantom. Her eyes were adjusting, but she wasn't sure she could trust them. And if she was able to make out his shadow, why couldn't he see her?

Because he's not looking at you, she thought, answering herself. He was assuming she was in bed, evident when he leaned and touched the duvet. But after a moment, the fabric ceased to rustle. She heard rather than saw his hand make a fist, gathering the material. Abruptly, he turned, glancing toward the door as if expecting to see her there, watching him.

Which she was. One hand gripped the bat, the fingers of the other pinched the lamp's chain. It felt flimsy between her damp fingers, as if it could snake from her tenuous grasp at any second.

She tugged.

The light snapped on.

Blinking hard against the sudden illumination, terrified because she couldn't see clearly, she used both hands to swing the bat backward, ready to strike the second she could locate her target. A hand had flown to his eyes to shield them— whether from the light, or from the bat's possible blow, she wasn't sure. Not that she cared what he was feeling at the moment, especially not when the hand lowered, her eyes adjusted, and she got a better look at his face.

"J.D.," she whispered, tightening her grip on the bat.

He said nothing. He sure didn't look like a ghost. So much for Mama Ambrosia's supposed connection to the supernatural world. As her eyes roved over each inch of him, she wanted to kill him, and yet, she wanted to kiss him, too, because no man had any right to be so damned sexy. His hair was as black as the night, wild with loose curls that licked around his forehead, dipping down into bushy black eyebrows that nearly met whenever he squinted, the way he was now. Fringed by a thick spray of inky lashes, his eyes were slashes of bright blue. Somehow they seemed to arc across his face like traces left by a streaking blue flame.

He wasn't quite beautiful. His nose had always kept him from being too pretty. It was long and craggy, with the kind of crook that had led plenty of people to assume he'd broken it repeatedly in bar fights, probably over a woman.

Intense was the word that best described her husband. His face was marred with premature character lines, lending him a world-weary expression, as if he was wise beyond his years, which of course he wasn't. Still, those eyes said his heart had been broken too many times already, but that he'd never quit loving—especially sexual loving—because it was as necessary to him as breathing.

Of course, in reality, J. D. Johnson was the real heartbreaker, a two-timing liar who excelled at hurting everyone he touched, especially Susannah.

Even now, coiled in his body, was the power that commanded crowds, an unnerving certainty, maybe even arrogance, as if to say he knew his questions would be answered and his desires satisfied. He still hadn't said a word, and she hadn't relinquished her hold on the bat. Her eyes settled on his mouth, which had remained as kissable as ever. It was smaller than one might have expected, especially given his singing voice and the wide, sculpted bones of his cheeks and jaw. His lips were usually pursed and cautious, just as they were right now, giving nothing away, and they were bracketed by a trim outcropping of mustache and artfully contrived stubble that served as a beard, dusting his chin…the same stubble that, no doubt, had left the red marks on her thighs last night.

Suddenly, she was glad she was wearing long pants, which at least hid the damage he'd done. If he saw the beard burns on her skin, she suspected he'd feel a certain sense of power, or worse, pride at the recollection of how she'd turned to putty under the ministrations of his mouth.

She swallowed hard, remembering how good that mouth could feel, and silently she cursed herself for it. He was gorgeous. The kind of man who'd look famous, even if a woman didn't know he was. And yet to her, he'd always be the guy she'd known since she was five…the guy who teased her in school, and whose folks owned the tackle shop in town.

He must have left his boots downstairs because he was barefoot. Otherwise, he was wearing a tight black T-shirt and ancient jeans that had faded to white. As she gazed at his lower body, she could swear she felt heat seeping through the fabric, although that was impossible.

She trailed her eyes upward again, praying that the surprise wasn't evident on her face, not wanting to give him that satisfaction. She fixed her gaze on his chest. For a long moment, she watched the rise and fall of enticing pectorals under the skin-hugging shirt. Finally she managed to say, "Well one thing's for certain, J. D. Johnson."

At the precise second she finished the words, her eyes raised another fraction and landed dead-center on his, her timing perfect. As if equally determined to feign nonchalance, he raised a black eyebrow in such a way that it arched and curled, as if trying to form a question mark. "What's that, Susannah Banner?" he drawled conversationally.

"You're still breathing," she said, her gaze flitting to his rising-falling chest once more.

"And?"

"Do you know what that means?" she asked sweetly.

"What?"

"That you're not dead," she said.

And then she swung the bat.

7

THWACK.

The bat smacked J.D.'s open palm, and he winced, cursing softly. The next few seconds seemed to last hours, maybe because so many impressions assaulted him at once. She'd broken his hand—that was his first thought, and that meant he couldn't play. Automatically he tallied the lost revenues he'd owe the professional musicians he performed with nowadays, and as he did, an image of his old band flashed into his mind. A pang of regret claimed his heart for not having seen them for ages.

Then J.D. remembered he was supposed to be dead, so his play dates had been canceled, anyway. Damn. How could he even think about music right now, or his old buddy when Susannah was standing in front of him? Why did he keep twisting his priorities? And how had he wound up losing his wife, the only thing he cared about?

When she'd swung the bat, she'd accidentally caught the lamp shade, and light from the bare bulb was shining directly into his eyes. Instinctively he flexed his fingers around the bat to protect himself from further assault, and when he did, he realized nothing was broken after all. He was just hurt, like his heart and hers.

He could see well enough to tell how she was glaring at

him, bracing her luscious legs, ready to fight. Not that he was going to let go of his end of her makeshift weapon. Still, it was the wrong time to think about how good those legs had felt wrapped tightly around his back last night.

She didn't look particularly surprised to see him, and *that* threw him for a loop. Maybe it shouldn't have. Susannah might not share his belief in the spirit world, but she'd often exhibited a sixth sense when it came to him, although she'd never admit it. Her flashing eyes said she'd suspected he was alive all along, and now that he'd confirmed her suspicions, her worst fears were being realized.

"I know you hate me," he managed to say, thinking that if he really loved her, he'd pivot on his heel and stride from the room without a backward glance. Surprised that his voice had sounded as raspy and sexy as a blues singer's, he wondered where the seduction came from—his longing to get out of the doghouse, or simply seeing Susannah up close for the first time in months. Last night he'd only teased and touched her in the dark, reveling in the feel of her smooth skin, the fluidity of curves that were as familiar to him as his own name. No matter how many songs he'd written, he'd never capture the rapture.

Capture the rapture. Now there was a rhyme worthy of another song about her. He'd written hundreds, maybe thousands. Recalling that, he gritted his teeth once more. Even when he should be using all his skills, searching for the right thing to say to her, he was creating lyrics about her instead....

Well no word or phrase could repair the damage now. Worse, he was still seeing spots and shadows. It was as if he were on stage. Night after night, far from home and lonely, he'd find himself staring into blinding white lights, the audiences beyond reduced to faceless shadows, which was just as well. He'd always been singing to Susannah, although she was never really there….

Even though he couldn't see her clearly, his blood thrummed, tunneling through his veins, ever faster, until it was whirring in his ears and pooling in his belly. He felt himself getting hard, his jeans tightening across his hips. No, he hadn't seen her up close for a while—it had been too long in fact—but he had watched her from afar. More than once, like a lovesick puppy, he'd lurked outside her restaurant in New York, praying he'd see her.

That's why he'd seen Joe, the man he'd overheard on the speaker phone last night. Sudden, unexpected anger coursed through him. Joe had brought a light to her eyes that J.D. had been sure he'd snuffed out, and in the restaurant, he'd watched her and Joe dance until helplessness and fury coiled in the pit of his stomach.

As he took in Susannah's wary expression, pain clawed inside him, and his lips pursed in frustrated, mute fury. He'd returned from his supposed grave to make peace, but all he wanted to do was hurt her for kissing the other man. Had she slept with him? He wouldn't blame her….

But Susannah was his! No other man's hands should touch her, certainly no other man's hard, hungry mouth. Abruptly, J.D. leaned, electricity skating along his arm when her skin grazed his. With a flick of his wrist, he righted the lamp shade, dimming the bulb so he could see, then he gripped his end of the bat harder and tugged. Clearly unwilling to relinquish her hold, she staggered forward a few steps, halting when she was close enough to share his body heat. His skin warmed, and his nostrils flared. The strong scent of her—all soft soap and hot musk—raced to his lungs.

His gut somersaulting, his heart hammering, he fought the

urge to drag her forcibly nearer, knowing he wouldn't rest until he did so. Already he could feel the soft cushioning of her full breasts, the hot catch of panting breath against his ear, the tendrils of silken hair teasing his cheeks, then the rush of heavenly contact when her pelvic bone ground between his legs. Just thinking about her intimate touch made something unexpected hit the back of his throat. His mouth went dry.

When his eyes settled on her moist mouth, he imagined the damp salve of her kiss as his tongue plundered, and when he looked into her blazing blue eyes, he imagined her gaze turning hotter on his naked body. She was so beautiful. Too damn beautiful. The kind of knocked-out, dragged-down, weak-in-the-knees, beautiful that could turn any reasonable man into a wild animal. One glance at her soft, pliable mouth and he wanted to hoot like an owl or howl like a wild beast at the moon.

He became restless, as if he'd never know another moment's peace until he was buried deep inside her, thrusting hard, moaning and groaning and sweating until his passion was spent. She hadn't said a word, and yet just one whisper of her sultry voice could bring him to his knees.

She knew it, too. No doubt, from where she stood, she could hear his heart pounding like a tribal drum. In the back of his mind, he was considering how much she weighed, how easy it would be to simply wrench the bat from her hand and haul her into his embrace. He saw himself turning, trapping her beneath him as he fell onto the bed they'd shared so many times. She'd like it, too. Oh, she'd make a show of fighting, maybe even hit him again, but he would win. He always did. Trouble was, J. D. Johnson was tired of winning, tired of wearing his wife down with sensual manipulations and calculated touches.

Now he wanted the impossible—for her to love him again. Or worse, for her to fall *in love* with him again. He wanted her to be head over heels, surrendering to him like some damsel in an old-fashioned swoon. And more, he wanted to deserve it. Wishful thinking, to be sure, because that was a closed chapter. Ancient history. Water under the bridge. Or at least a flowing river of the good scotch whiskey he used to drink. In truth, if he was lucky, maybe the love of his life would let him deliver his apology before she tried to hit him with the bat again.

Then he'd vanish.

He had it all planned out. He'd melt into the night like a phantom, into the darkness he deserved for making such a wretched mess of their lives.

But now that he'd touched her, he couldn't move. He told himself to forget the apology and leave before he hurt her more, but he was anchored to the spot.

He could still identify remnants of the little girl she'd once been. He could remember each of the countless freckles that had once sprinkled her nose, then faded in bygone days, and how her chubby cheeks had hollowed, creating the angular planes and high cheekbones over which his gaze now roved. Her mama and daddy were gone, and once, she'd told him she loved him because he was one of the few who would always remember her childhood. "In that way, you're like Mama and Daddy rolled into one, J.D.," she'd said.

She was thinner now, which wasn't good—probably from working too hard at her restaurant. But her eyes were steady, her chin rigid, her shoulders squared. Everything about her said, "nobody's doormat." Her nose was long and straight, lending her a patrician air suitable to the Banner name of which she'd always been so proud. It was a name she'd sought to protect, but he'd only run roughshod over it, ruining her heritage with all his drinking and carrying on. She even thought he'd slept with another woman.

Which was why she'd never forgive him. Shadows had begun to dance over her cheeks, making her eyelashes look impossibly long, just like the shadow of her figure that nearly touched the ceiling behind her. Usually lively, her blue eyes were watchful now, more steely than the usual blazing blue of fire.

Her face was chalk-white, as if she'd seen a ghost. Her mouth was a very tempting pink, inviting the sort of relentless kiss that would lead to more. "You don't look surprised to see me," he finally murmured.

"Would it be better if I was?"

Maybe not. He could barely find his voice, and once more he damned himself for putting people through what he had. Everything had happened so quickly and he'd had no time to think. "No," he finally said in a near whisper.

"I had a gut feeling something was fishy," she burst out. "I didn't tell anybody what I secretly suspected—they'd think I was crazy. They'd think I'd gotten fanciful, the way Mama did sometimes. What's going on, J.D.?"

"I can explain."

"Why would I want to hear your explanations?"

"You just asked."

"I guess I did, so you'd better talk fast."

Twisting the bat quickly, he tried to wrench it from her grasp, but she only reclaimed it, swinging it to her side. He felt strangely bereft, with the small connection between them severed. A second ago, he could have sworn he'd felt her pulse traveling along the wood, could have sworn his own heart was beating in tandem with it. "C'mon, Susannah, you don't want to hit me," he said quietly.

"Wrong, J.D. I already tried. And it would feel really good to do it again."

"Well, if you're still mad, maybe you care."

"You wish." He sensed, rather than saw her grip tighten on the bat again. "You bastard," she suddenly added, her eyes flashing. "You've pulled plenty of self-centered stunts in your lifetime, Jeremiah Dashiell, but this takes the cake. What brought on the sick urge to attend your own funeral?"

Her lips clamped together, and he figured she'd just remembered how she'd wept during the service, holding his fool hunting cap. Before he thought it through, he lifted his hand, brought it to her face and trailed a finger down her cheek, but she veered back, as if his touch stung. In the second before she broke contact, he could swear he saw her chin quiver, but now it looked as hard as granite.

Somehow that hurt the most. He knew she still had feelings for him. For two weeks, he'd been spying on her, so he'd watched her cry, wandering Banner Manor like some mourning Victorian maiden while she sorted through his stuff. "It's a long story," he finally forced himself to say.

"Let me guess. You wanted to see who cried the most?" Her voice lowered. "Did I win? Are you happy now?"

Memories flooded him, and for a moment he couldn't breathe. "Maybe," he said. "I guess I didn't figure anyone would cry at all."

"Satisfied?"

"Not really."

It wasn't what he'd meant to say. Somehow, the conversation was going all wrong. Outside, standing under the windows, watching her from the trees, he'd been practicing a heartfelt speech. But now it seemed useless. Probably because, for the first time in his life, J.D. had no clue what he wanted. The night the boat had blown up, he'd had only one thought: to escape everything in his old life and to try to get Susannah back. But that was impossible….

He tried to focus on what he'd come to say. "The explosion," he began simply, his thoughts jumbled because he was looking at he prettiest face he'd ever seen. Shaking his head, he vaguely wondered how he could write lyrics that made other women swoon and yet become tongue-tied the second he tried to talk to his own wife.

"I was driving to meet you," he began. She glanced away, and he watched her gaze flit from place to place, as if to say anything in the room was more interesting than him. "I thought…hoped…you might meet me on the *Alabama*, the way you said."

Pausing, he shrugged, hoping to find words that would explain the confusion of that night. His friends had still been at the house, but they'd been packing and clearing out. Even Maureen was gone. When Susannah had found Sandy in bed with him, he'd asked *her* to leave, and she had, but she'd come back that day, saying she'd left a bag she had to find.

Trying to concentrate on what was most important, he continued, "I was on the way to meet you, but my truck ran out of gas."

"Out of gas," Susannah repeated, shaking her head, her hair looking as soft and golden as an angel's halo. "I know. They found your truck by the road. And these are just the kind of rambling excuses I should have expected. You pretend to be dead, then come in here, talking about how you ran out of gas. Damn you, J.D.," she huffed. "You're just not normal."

She was right. He wasn't. He'd been a lousy husband, too, forgetting anniversaries and birthdays and family dinners. He hadn't protected their niece, Laurie, either, although she had been his responsibility. "I'm a bastard, Susannah," he said, dragging a hand through his hair, not that the gesture relieved any frustration. "A nasty, selfish SOB who's driven everything I've loved into the ground. I admit it."

"And you rose from your grave just to tell me that? I don't need a ghost to explain it. I could have asked anybody in Bayou Banner."

Once more, he could barely find his voice. "Seemed like you were worth coming back for."

"Maybe some things are better left buried."

"Like me? Our marriage?" Tears weren't even shimmering in her eyes. She'd hardened her heart to him. Since she remained silent, he continued, "So you can cry for me if I'm dead, but not alive?"

"If you vanish for good, we can find out."

As he watched her, he no longer knew why he was here. He told himself to turn and leave, but he simply couldn't. "My truck ran out of gas, like I said, but I was sure I filled the tank. Nobody else could have driven my truck, either." Shaking his head, he thought back to the long, dark stretch of road near the river. "When it died—"

"That's not the only thing that died," she interjected.

He ignored the comment. "Just listen for once. I got out of the truck and started running, Susannah. I was almost there, about a half mile from the marina and the dock, when I realized somebody had taken out the *Alabama*. I thought maybe you—"

"An attendant said he saw you onboard."

"Wasn't me."

"You thought I'd really come to meet you? You're so arrogant! While you're on the road, do groupie girls fall for your pack of lies—"

"There are no girls!"

"You always think you'll get your way!" she shouted. "It's always whatever J.D. wants, whenever he wants it."

"Yeah, it was wishful thinking that you'd come meet me," he managed. "But you never give me an inch, either, Susannah."

"An inch? You take miles!"

His eyes willed her to understand. "I was staring at the boat when it blew. Everything went sky-high. Sparks shot into the air, then flames. Debris was flying. I...think I must have gone into shock or something. Just for a second. I'm not sure what happened after that. At some point, I realized I'd just kept running." His voice broke. "I was sure that you were..."

"Dead?"

"Yeah."

"The way you pretended to be?"

Pain knifed into him. Dammit, how could he have put people through the past two weeks after what he'd felt in that moment? "I was going to call you. Garrison had called before to say you weren't coming, but I didn't believe him. I knew you loved me...believed in us...would change your mind. But then I called, and you picked up the phone and I knew..."

"I wasn't coming?"

"And that it was over...*we* were over." Even now, he could see the flames shooting out of the boat like arrows, illuminating the trees. Leaves were blowing wildly from the surge of the blast. "I hung up on you and ran. The boat was sinking fast—it went down before I could get to the river."

One second, the *Alabama* was coasting in the water—sleek and clean and beautiful, skimming a barely rippling surface that looked as smooth as glass—and the next, the boat was gone. What was left of the craft upended and slipped beneath the wake. A strong swimmer, he'd run to the water's edge, and could still feel his boot heels pushing off the sandy bank as he barreled toward the water.

He'd dived repeatedly, holding his breath as long as he could, then coming up for air, trying to find anyone, thinking maybe whoever had been aboard had been thrown clear of the wreckage. All along he'd feared maybe someone had been injured or sunk to the bottom. The river was deep and dark, home to snakes and gators, the bed strewn with sharp rocks and tendrils of vines that had wound around his legs, clinging.

"After a while—I don't know how long—I heard voices on shore."

"You don't know how long? Just how much had you been drinking, J.D.?"

"Some, Susannah."

"And driving?"

"I wasn't drunk," he defended. But the truth was, he wasn't really sure. There was nothing like whiskey to make the world go away, which was why he'd been hitting the bottle pretty regularly, but he was done with all that. She had to believe him. The booze had just been the dress rehearsal for the main event, which was when he'd walked out of his own life. Now *that* had been the greatest escape.

"I recognized Sheriff Kemp's voice," he said, "and I realized he'd shown up with guys in diving gear. They were already going in."

"And you…"

"Slipped onto the opposite bank and left." He shook his head, once more wondering what to tell her. He'd share anything, of course. She'd always been his confessor, privy to his deepest, darkest secrets, but now his own actions and motivations were a mystery to him, so he didn't know what to say. "C'mon, Susannah," he finally whispered, stepping forward a pace to close the gap between them.

She leaned back, and he instinctively reached, gripping her upper arm. As his fingers possessively circled her flesh, he drew her near, her scent shooting to his lungs again. His body moving of its own unconscious volition, he leaned and pressed his face to her hair, inhaling deeply, and for the briefest moment, the world stopped spinning.

Everything was utterly still. No breath, no heartbeat. Just him and her, alone in the world, with no one to bother them. Surprisingly, she let him nuzzle, and his arms ached to wrap around her so tightly that she could never escape. He wanted to take her away with him, where they could be alone....

He tried to steady himself, but he still felt dizzy. He needed more of her...needed to thrust his hands into her hair and spiral his fingers into the waving curls that were the color of hand-spun golden sunlight mixed with honey. How many times had he awakened with that hair fanning his bare chest? How many times had he finger-combed the silken strands while she breathed softly, her mind lost to dreams?

His leg was pressed hard against the mattress and suddenly he was aware of the bed, and of how Susannah's breasts swayed under her T-shirt. He could make out the sloping flesh, the contours of the nipples, and he visualized them—soft, pink, relaxed, full, ready for his mouth. His groin ached, the sensation of longing undeniable. It was like a craving for a drug, something that just kept coming at him, demanding action.

He thought about last night—the sweet, salty taste of her—and how she'd responded. And he remembered how she'd called him Joe.

But *he'd* been her lover. He wanted her to know it, too. He wanted to strip off her clothes and remind her of why they'd kept loving each other all these years, through thick and thin. He could remember her soft voice uttering their wedding vows, *for richer, for poorer, in sickness and in health.*

"I just took off that night," he found himself saying, his voice husky. "I knew Sheriff Kemp's men were better equipped to keep diving. I just started walking, cut through the woods." He'd been drenched and shivering. "I wound up at Mama Ambrosia's. She put me up for the night. Plied me with some herbal concoction, too." Ever since, he'd wondered what kind of spell she'd cast on him, not that he figured even her most potent charms could reverse all the lousy luck he kept bringing on himself.

"That charlatan! She's been calling here, saying I should expect a visit from your ghost. She knew all along...."

"Oh no," he muttered.

"And where are you staying now?"

"For a while, I went to an abandoned cabin down the bayou, and then I..." His voice trailed off. "Oh, forget it. Does it matter?"

"No."

His grip on her arm loosened, because he knew better than to do what he wanted, which was to rub slow, sensual circles on her skin. If she came an inch nearer, he couldn't vouch for what he'd do. He'd missed her so much. "I wasn't thinking—"

"You never do, J.D.! That's my point!"

"I had to get away. To think."

"Your parents!"

"I called them. Then I went to see them. They know I'm all right."

"When?"

"A few days ago."

Now she did hit him again. She raised a hand, hauled it

back and punched him. What bothered him most was the in-effectual way the blow connected with his chest, not really hurting at all. He wished it had. He could have taken another whack of the bat, too. Or a slap in the face. But the sissy's smack wasn't Susannah's style. He'd wounded her, weakened her. He could see that now. And it was the last thing he'd ever wanted to do. Susannah was born strong and tough, more than she knew.

"You told your parents you were alive, but not me?"

"I wanted to tell you myself."

"They didn't call me?"

"They wanted to."

"You stopped them."

How could he explain? "I…watched you for days," he said, his voice sounding faraway and gravelly, like something made from scrap metal or rusted tin. "I saw you wandering through the house in agony, and I just couldn't decide which was worse—telling you that I was still around, or just doing you a favor and disappearing forever."

From the expression on at her face, he wished he'd done the latter. That's what she'd have wanted. He understood that now. Later, he figured she'd learn to love some other man. She seemed to like Joe. "I thought…you'd be better off without me. Maybe if I just vanished…"

"You wanted off the hook. Out of our marriage!"

"That's a lie!"

"You wanted to sleep with all those groupies!"

"Not so. That's your own baggage, Susannah. Your fears and your jealousy."

"Oh please! Fess up to it, J.D.!"

"I won't, because it's a lie." Steel was in his voice, thread-ing through his words. "There was a time I wanted success," he continued, biting out the words. "I've never not admitted that. The lure of fame was strong. What man wouldn't want it?" Girls had been all over him. Producers telling him he was far more talented than he really was. Men fawning, hanging onto his every word because he had the power to help them in their own careers. His family had never had much money, but suddenly he could buy anything he wanted.

"I was weak," he managed. "But I didn't know how—"

"How what?" she interjected, scoffing. "To live your own life? And so you took the first opportunity to walk out of it? Once more, J. D. Johnson chooses the easy way! Why am I not surprised? But this time you had the nerve to pretend you were dead!"

Reeling back, she broke free of his grasp. "June," she suddenly said with horror. "Clive. The girls." She shook her head as if memories of the funeral were flooding back to her. "Laurie was heartbroken. Ellie and Robby. Everybody in town. That publicist tried to make a circus out of the funeral. Robby could barely fight her off."

"I'm sorry," he said softly.

"You drive around in that truck, half-drunk, running traffic lights in town," she said, speaking as if she were verbalizing a rant she'd often had in her own head. "It's amazing you haven't done more damage than this!" She gasped. "And *who* was on the boat?" Her eyes widened. "Somebody else was on it! It wasn't me, the way you thought. Or you. But there was a body. They said it was…"

"Unrecognizable?"

She nodded.

"I don't know who it was. But I'll find out. I swear I will, Susannah." He reached for her once more, settling a hand on her shoulder, the touch so possessive that he dared her to pull away. "I haven't had a drink since that night. I want you to know that. I'm going to make everything right, I swear."

She merely shook her head again. "You break everybody's heart and now you want brownie points for apologies?"

"No."

"Then what?" Her voice cracked. "Why did you come back?"

"Are you going to deny that we belong together?" Stepping closer, he wedged a thigh between hers. "I can handle your anger, Susannah," he murmured softly, his breath catching as he drew in her scent. "Even your hate. In fact, I can handle anything you throw at me."

"Why did you come back?"

"For this, damn you." Abruptly his mouth swept hers. "And this." His lips settled, firm and moist, raw and searing. They molded to hers, just long enough to experience the sweet pressure and escalating heat. He whispered, "And because I've been watching you."

Her head veered back, but he grabbed her, holding her close. Inches away, her eyes lit into his like lasers. Blue on blue, fire to fire. "You were spying? I bet you loved doing that, J.D."

"Of course I didn't."

"Oh, yes, you did," she accused. "Your ego has loved every minute of the past two weeks. The eulogies. The music. The flowers. Everybody's tears."

"Screw you, Susannah," he bit out, a sudden surge of anger barely restrained. "You act like I'm the only one who plays games with emotions."

"Aren't you?"

"No. And sometimes, I never want to try to share mine with you again. Maybe I won't. Not tonight. Not ever. It killed me to watch my own funeral."

He'd been so sure nobody cared about him anymore. He'd

been surrounded by false friends. Susannah had walked out on him. His best buddy, Robby, wasn't exactly hanging around anymore. Ellie had always sided with Susannah, which meant she'd been treating him like a two-timing pariah, which he wasn't, then she'd left town, his wife in tow.

"You know me well enough to know I didn't mean to upset you."

"No, I don't think I know you at all, J.D."

It was the meanest thing she could have said, but he barely heard her. He was still thinking about his funeral. He could see the whole scene: His folks crying. Little Laurie, his niece, looking contrite as a nun and all straightened out, wearing a trim navy suit as if she were going to a tryout for the Junior League. He'd been so happy to see her in a decent outfit that he was truly glad he'd passed to the next life.

For months, he'd only seen Laurie wear ripped black dresses and trashy fishnet stockings. Susannah had been clutching the hunting hat she professed to hate so much and wearing dark sunglasses to hide her eyes. His parents were stoic, which was how they dealt with things. Delia and Sheriff Kemp were side by side, so J.D. figured the man had finally asked her out.

Some of J.D.'s newer friends had tried to come, and although he and Robby weren't speaking much, Robby had run them off, just the way a best buddy would. He hadn't seen the gorgeous chick, Sandy, the one who dated Joel, and who had been in bed with him, but Maureen, the publicist, was there. Hidden by an outcropping, and watching the service through a window, J.D. could only marvel at how much he'd destroyed the great life that had once been his. He'd known the world's best people, truly the salt of the earth, and he'd blown it.

"That day, I realized you might miss me, Susannah." It was the first time he'd been honestly sure she might. "More than you're admitting right now."

"Well, I don't."

"Liar," he managed. She knew which buttons to push, but he was determined not to react. When the boat blew, he'd been half blinded with emotion. Even after he'd been assured that she was okay, he'd remained scared that Susannah had been on board. At that moment, life had seemed fleeting.

So he'd acted on impulse, with no thought of the consequences. He'd just wanted to remove everything Susannah hated from their lives. Vaguely he'd thought he could turn himself around, quit drinking, get rid of his so-called friends, then get her back. And so he'd walked away.

"I didn't even realize people would believe I was on the boat," he explained. "After I left Mama Ambrosia's, I went to an abandoned cabin and I nursed myself off the booze. By the time I figured out I was supposed to be dead, my funeral had already been planned."

"There were remains," Susannah whispered.

"Somebody else's. Like I said, I don't know whose."

"And you?"

"Took off. I've been wandering around like a ghost for weeks. I thought you might be better off if I…"

"Never came back?"

"Yeah."

"But you spied on me?"

"I heard you through the windows last night, talking to Joe. And I saw you with him in New York."

She gasped. "In New York?"

"A couple of times before…uh, before the accident."

"Why?"

"I was thinking about you. That's for sure. I dressed in a

disguise, a hat and glasses. I like what you did in your restaurant…." Pausing, he cursed softly, the word scarcely audible. "That's an understatement! I was proud of you, Susannah. I'm not finding the right words. I never do with you. I can write songs, but when I talk to you, sometimes… Anyway, I always knew you wanted to do great things in life. And when I saw how you decorated the restaurant, I…"

"What?"

"Hated myself even more. You decorated it the way you'd planned to do our house, all the things you used to talk about—the drapes, tablecloths, curtains. I realized the only reason you'd never done it was because of me and the people who were staying here."

"About those people," she said coldly.

She'd accepted the brush of his lips a moment ago. She hadn't responded, but she hadn't pulled away. But he realized that might well be their very last kiss. Ever. Pain seared through him like a knife. How could he live without loving her?

"I never slept with her, Susannah," he suddenly said.

"She was in our bed."

The same bed that was right beside them, the duvet already turned down, the sheets inviting. "She got into bed with me after I fell asleep. She said she'd been partying, thought she was in another room with Joel. Nothing happened."

"Passed out would be a more accurate phrase."

"I won't argue with that."

"Then I guess we're fresh out of things to say."

"How could we be? What other two people can talk like us, Susannah? I know my tongue gets tied sometimes, but think of the songs I've written for you. And how many nights have we lain awake talking until dawn?"

"Don't try to sweet-talk me."

It was his only chance. "The restaurant was incredible," he forced himself to continue. "You've...done so much better without me. You look good." Suddenly his throat was aching again. "And Joe. He seems like a nice guy. He really does. Attentive, unlike me. He was listening to every word you said."

"And what else do you know about him?"

"Just what I saw when you were talking in the restaurant, and last night on the phone."

"Through the window?"

"The French doors were open, too."

"I knew I felt someone watching me!"

"I wanted to come inside, to say something to you. I was thinking about it when the phone rang. I didn't mean to eavesdrop. I know I've ruined everything. You don't have to tell me. Maybe you can't love me anymore. I don't even care what you did with...with him," he managed to say.

It was a lie. The thought of another man helping Susannah orgasm made him feel as if he'd just been sucker-punched. Or mortally wounded. At the though, he wanted to double over in agony. But she needed love. Care. Decency and respect. Someone with whom to share life's ups and downs. All the things he'd been so lousy at providing.

"My life is none of your business, J.D."

Technically it was. They were still married, but he was smart enough to know this it was the wrong time to point that out. "I want you to be happy."

"So you drank like a fish, brought crazy people into my house, left the scene of an explosion, where somebody apparently died, then pretended to be dead yourself—"

She shouldn't have looked so sexy right then. She was sleep-rumpled and every time he looked at her he remembered what happened last night. Once more, he wanted to trail his tongue over every inch of her body until she writhed and moaned. He wanted to kiss her until she swore she hadn't really enjoyed anything Joe O'Grady had done to her.

Abruptly, he tightened his grip on her and dragged her close. Her lips were a mere inch away, the lower one quivering. Her eyes were unblinking and unforgiving, but she wanted him to kiss her again. He'd known her for years, so he knew she was waiting for it. Angling his head, he leaned a fraction nearer so their mouths nearly touched, but then he couldn't bring himself to give her—or himself—the satisfaction. No, he wanted her to admit she still cared, still wanted him, still craved his kiss.

"You've got me twisted in knots again. You always do. One look at you and I lose my head, or act like a fool, or do stupid things like walk away from an explosion."

"Don't blame me for your actions," she warned.

"I'm not. I'm just trying to say there's no escape. For better or worse, Susannah. For richer, for poorer."

"In your fantasies. People divorce all the time, J.D. Fifty percent of the lucky population, in fact. And I signed my papers months ago. Besides, weren't you going to get that post-nuptial?"

"I never agreed to that."

"Maybe you should have!"

"Because we're divorcing?"

"Not anymore. You're dead. Remember?"

"Not so dead I can't feel this," he insisted right before his lips found their mark. Just that flare of heat and spark was enough to make him lose control. Suddenly, his warring emotions surged. He hated her as much as he loved her. Hated her because she was withholding her body. Loved her because he simply did. He always would.

He sank into the kiss. Drowned. His lips parted with hers, and he was at the bottom of the river once more, diving into the black swirling depths, swept away by wild, racing currents. His tongue thrust hard, then harder, the kiss all-consuming because he was sure it might be their last. It thrilled him to realize she was kissing him back, too. The first touch of her tongue was slow, exploratory and tentative, as if against her will.

Dragging her down to the bed, he did what he'd been thinking about since the first moment he'd seen her. Rolling fluidly on top of her, as he'd done a thousand times before, he whispered, "You're right. I'm dead. As far as the world knows, I'm gone, Susannah. So it's just you and me. No one else. No concerts. No publicists. No groupies and musicians. No one to come between us."

She planted her hands on his chest and pushed. "You have to come clean. Your fans wrote sympathy cards. I read them. Apologize."

"I am. To you first. I wish I'd never learned to play," he said, whispering the words against her cheek. "I wish I had just gone to work in Dad's shop, the way we figured I would. I hate everything that's separated us."

"You can't waltz in and take back years."

"I did last night," he reminded.

When she tried to pull away, he held tight, his heart pounding harder with every flicker of his tongue on her skin, because he wanted to devour it, smothering each inch with kisses. "What did you think last night? Did you remember this morning? Did you ever think it was me?" he whispered. "I heard you use Joe's name, but did you really think another man could love your body the way I do?"

"You heard Joe's name and left?"

"Yeah."

"I thought I was dreaming," she admitted, her voice hitching, reminding him of how much he loved it. It was soft and sweet and lilted like an Irish lullaby, making him want to sing.

"You weren't dreaming," he assured her, gently tonguing her ear. "And it wasn't him. It was me…"

"I went to see Mama Ambrosia today," she said as she let him continue kissing her neck, as if she might actually let him make love to her. "She said your ghost was going to haunt me."

He shifted his weight and poised his mouth above hers, hovering. Her body tensed now, as if for she was debating between fight or flight, but she was trapped beneath him. Nibbling, he feathered the gentlest of kisses across her lips. "Let me haunt you," he whispered.

"No, J.D."

"Yes." His mouth covered hers once more. The kiss flared, sparked, sizzled, then burned. Her hungry mouth clung, and to make her respond more fully, he used his knee to part her thighs and let his hips fall between them. Relief filled him, his whole body sighing as he enjoyed the familiarity of their joining. His hands thrust upward, the fingers splayed, rushing into her hair. Fisting the strands, he dragged her mouth closer and moaned.

"Let me shanghai you, Susannah," he muttered as his tongue swept wetly across her lips. "Kidnap you and take you to a forgotten cabin," he whispered, his tongue thrusting now, plunging. "Or maybe to the rocky, windswept shore of some faraway island. Anywhere but here. Let's go where there are no memories of us fighting. Come with me and hide from the world."

"You're good with words, J.D.," she whispered.

It implied his actions never measured up. Still, his breath caught, since she was his again, if only for a moment. She needed him desperately. Memories of her nails digging into his shoulders the previous night caused a visceral thrill as his mouth assaulted hers once more, his tongue pushing ever deeper between her lips. Lightly, he tugged once more on her water-soft hair, stroking her scalp, knowing how it affected her, until she tilted her head and uttered a series of cooing cries.

Yes…she was his now. They were going all the way. As he deepened the kiss, his own cry of need stifled in his throat. He'd never wanted anything as badly as he wanted her now. The kiss turned languid, slow and unbelievably wet.

"This is what I came for," he murmured. Warmth broke over his skin. His erection felt heavy, his jeans impossibly tight. Shifting his weight, he inched upward, climbing higher between her legs, gasping when her pelvis chaffed his zipper, the feeling torturous and intense. He feared he'd come without even being inside her, but he was powerless except to move against her anyway, his mind exploding as he melted into the heavenly heat he could feel through her clothes.

Far gone, he let his tongue stroke down the length of her's, the tip flickering like butterflies' wings, until they were both panting hard. His chest constricted. He was aching, so hot that he couldn't stand it one more minute. Slanting his mouth across hers again and again, he muttered between kisses, "Doesn't it feel good? Don't you want it?"

When she didn't respond, he reached down, catching the hem of her shirt. Pushing it roughly upward, he rustled his fingers beneath. She gasped as he opened his mouth wider, sweeping his tongue against the slick interior of her cheek, then he cupped a breast, squeezed and kneaded. A second later, his fingers rushed to the nipple. Molten fire shooting to his loins, he registered the tautness of the bud. Rapidly he rubbed, his nails playing with the excited tip.

As he toyed, she bucked, her hips suddenly twitching and

wild, wrenching and seeking. Fire touched fire. As fast as lightning, he responded, his hips grinding, his buttocks tightening. Her mouth assaulted his, tussling back, and his tongue thrust blindly, his mind empty. Feeling her chest heave, he felt his heart singing.

She still loved him. And he loved her. He was throbbing, about to explode in his jeans. Momentarily he thought he really might, the way he had years ago when they were teenagers, before they'd had the nerve to sleep together. Back then, she'd tease him. She'd stroke him through his jeans and curl her fingers around the aroused length until he was mad with lust. And then one day, she'd finally unzipped his fly….

He raised himself on an elbow, careful not to break their kiss. Years ago, she'd been tentative and unsure, but so eager to please him. She had, too. Beyond his wildest dreams. And now he was going to return the favor.

Sliding his splayed hand down the silken skin of her ribs, he reached between them and undid the snap of his pants. Her open mouth captured his frustrated sigh as he jerked the zipper downward, over his erection. Glad he hadn't worn a belt, he pushed the denim over his hips just a fraction before he found her waistband and pulled down her pants.

When flesh met flesh, his frustration climbed, since ecstasy was now within reach. He was throbbing against her, burning, and in just a second, he'd be inside. He'd feel release.

"Oh, J.D." she sighed.

Hearing her words, his heart felt as if it were tumbling like a star from the sky. A brick from a tower. He had a dazed feeling, as if a rug had been snatched out from under him. "Susannah," he whispered, panting.

But she was pushing his shoulders again, twisting from under him. He reached too late as she scrambled to her feet. As he rolled over, he caught her leaning to grab the bat once more.

Her voice was shaking. "Get out before I call Sheriff Kemp. You're supposed to be dead, so maybe it's better if you stay that way, J.D. I'm not falling for sweet talk. Do you know how many people you've hurt? Not just me, J.D. And the past still exists. You can't erase it. Not tonight. Not ever."

Her mouth was the color of shiny rubies. Her T-shirt was raised on one side, almost enough to expose her breasts. They were visibly aroused, the nipples pert and straining against the cotton. Just seeing that, another wave of heat poured into his groin. His eyes trailed downward, and for the first time, he realized she was still wearing her wedding ring.

So was he. Not that he cared. His whole focus was how she'd affected him physically.

Somehow, he stood. His heart hammering, he yanked the zipper halfway over his truly bothersome erection, uttering a soft grunt of frustrated protest. Leaving the snap undone, he walked toward her. "Say you love me, Susannah. Say you miss me. That you forgive me. I know we can start over. Say you'll help me make our lives right again."

She smacked his cheek. The blow stung, but not nearly as much as the judgment in her eyes. "You can't play with people's emotions, J.D. I was angry enough to divorce you before, but this? People were devastated!"

"*You* were devastated," he corrected.

"Not anymore"

Once more, anger shot through him. "It hasn't been easy to have so much change in our lives, Susannah. My career and the fame has been a rush. Unexpected. More than we dreamed of. But where have you been? Supporting me?"

"You're a hard man to support."

He was hard. That much was certain. Every last nerve in his body was sizzling, craving her. "Maybe. But I'm not nearly the bad boy you make me out to be," he assured her, reaching for her again. This time, his hand cupped her face, his fingers curling under her chin. "You've been scared, but you'll never admit it."

She gaped at him. "Scared?"

"Yeah. Scared I'd run off with some girl in another town while I'm playing music, or that my fast life would become more interesting than you. That's why you keep accusing me of sleeping around, even though you know I never would. That woman, Sandy, got into bed with me. I was sleeping. And that's all."

"Just leave, J.D. I have to get my beauty rest. First thing tomorrow morning, I'm flying to New York to attend an awards ceremony, since my dead husband can't accept his prize if he wins."

His lips parted in surprise. He'd forgotten all about the awards. "You don't have to do that."

"I wouldn't miss it for the world. The lights. The cameras. The action." She glared at him. "A million reminders of the life I never wanted to live."

"Then go ahead and torture yourself."

"Gladly. But I'd rather do it alone."

"Have it your way. But you're the one who needs to 'fess up. I've supposedly always been the bad boy, which leaves you in the position to be the good girl. But one day, when I'm gone, you're going to have to take a better look at yourself."

He pivoted then, vaguely realizing that nothing had gone as he'd hoped. He walked out of the room and into the hallway, then down the stairs of his home for what might be the last time, but not a thing had been resolved between him and Susannah.

At the front door, he finally managed to snap his jeans closed. Then he flicked on a light, glanced at his guitar rack, some picks on the mantle and posters made from his CDs.

All the objects seemed to have been taken from another man's life. Maybe because without Susannah, none of them mattered. All his accomplishments seemed as if they'd been he'd done a million years ago. Was he really about to walk out the door and away from his life? Again?

He glanced up the stairs for a hopeful second, but she hadn't followed. She knew he was alive, and she didn't care if he lived or died. Oh, he'd seen the spark in her eyes, and felt the raw lust in her kisses, but the real love, whatever could fix the completely unfixable in life…well, that was gone, snuffed out like a candle that had once burned brightly.

As he leaned to pull on boots he'd left near the door, he squinted. *Sandy*, he suddenly thought. There was a small pink duffel near the door, half buried by a pile of his music books. The duffel was barely big enough to hold a couple pairs of jeans, but he was sure it belonged to her.

After Susannah had discovered her in bed with him, he'd asked Sandy to leave. She'd been incredibly apologetic, even offering to explain things to Susannah, claiming she'd been partying and was so tired that she'd wound up in the wrong room, thinking J.D. was her friend, Joel. Not that J.D. had believed her. He sensed something duplicitous, but still wasn't sure why.

Recalling the conversation made J.D. cringe. As he'd talked to her—looking past her beauty to the gaunt figure and vacant gray eyes—he wondered how he'd brought a person such as her into his and Susannah's lives, however accidentally. Why hadn't he noticed how the woman looked before? Not tall and slender, but almost waif-like? Joel, the man she'd come with, was a talented musician, but he was a loser in every other aspect of his life, a man who'd alienated his family and lived for the road. The kind of man J.D. was becoming…

He cursed under his breath. And to think little Laurie almost slept with the man. As it turned out, Joel and Sandy weren't even that close. After she'd gone, Joel was distressed, but Sandy had seemed to leave him without fanfare. It was strange. The last time J.D. had seen her was on the day of the explosion. He'd been alone in the house; she said she'd forgotten some of her things, but if so, why hadn't she taken the duffel? Had she not been able to find it?

What if she returned to ask Susannah for it? Preferring the bag not be found here, he grabbed the strap and lifted it onto his shoulder. As light as it was, it felt heavy, a reminder of how he'd lost Susannah. Still, he had to get going and couldn't leave it.

Opening the front door, he crossed the threshold to the porch and realized he was again straining his ears, hoping to hear Susannah's voice, yelling, "Wait a minute, J.D."

Digging into his pocket, he withdrew the house key he'd used for years. His hand trembled slightly as he placed it on a table beside the door. A moment later, the door shut firmly behind him, locking him out of his home, away from his wife.

And then he did the right thing—freed Susannah—and vanished into the night.

8

As THE FRONT DOOR CLOSED, Susannah realized her hand was pressed over her racing heart. Her lips felt swollen from J.D.'s kisses and her breasts were sore from wanting his touch. The delicious crush of his taut body had left her belly jittery, and she reached for the bedside table to steady herself.

Leave it to J.D.! He'd wound her up and made her as breathless as a groupie. Exhaling a shuddering sigh, Susannah tried to get her bearings, but the world seemed to tilt, shifting on its axis. At seeing her husband alive, she'd been more shocked than she'd let on, and thankfully he'd misread her stunned stupor.

"He *would*," she muttered furiously. He was the same old J.D. all right, more concerned about himself than anyone else, especially her. From the second she'd laid eyes on him, though, she'd realized she'd never been convinced he was gone, not deep down. Oh, she'd believed it at the funeral, she supposed. Why wouldn't she trust the sheriff and Robby? She'd been too distraught to ask questions, so she'd trusted everyone else to make the arrangements.

But something had always niggled, like a sixth sense, telling her he wasn't really gone. She'd put one foot in front of the other, anyway—mechanically getting on the plane with Ellie, numbly choosing an outfit for the funeral, cleaning the house. But she'd known the truth. And not just because Mama Ambrosia had started calling, acting as if she possessed inside information about J.D.'s death, which, as things turned out, she had.

"No wonder that charlatan left town," Susannah whispered. "Why, she must have been trying to make me look for J.D., trying to get us back together since she knew the truth." J.D. had probably given Mama a sob story about wanting Susannah back.

Not a believer in the paranormal, Susannah had written off her premonitions, thinking they were due to her being mad at J.D. After all, how could fate let the most annoying man in the world die before Susannah had given him a final piece of her mind?

Of course, now that she'd told him off, she didn't feel quite satisfied. Had he really announced that *she*, not he, had been the problem with their marriage? As if she were insecure! Or afraid scantily clad young women could excite him more than she! It was just like J.D. to pull some mind-blowing, self-centered stunt, then come swaggering in, blaming her!

Now her every last nerve was itching to chase him down and finish the argument! Not that she gave a rat's ass about J.D. In fact, she hated him more than mice hated cats, or cats hated dogs, or dogs hated rain. They'd been stuck together as if glued, true enough, but lately, they'd become fire and water, raw elements that could never mix and survive.

She just wished his lips hadn't felt so good, nibbling her skin, landing on her mouth and tasting as sweet as chocolate. A cry escaped from between her lips. How could her fool husband still be alive? She'd been so sure she'd never feel his heavenly touch again....

Had he really quit drinking, the way he claimed? Had he changed? Wouldn't she be a fool if she believed him one more time? Finally, who had been on the *Alabama* if it hadn't been J.D.?

One thing was certain. Somebody had been on the boat, and the poor soul hadn't escaped the fiery inferno. Was someone—a lover or friend—fretting about that missing person, wondering why he or she hadn't come home? Had their opportunity to grieve been taken away? Would J.D. discover the person's identity as he'd promised?

Telling herself she was motivated by civic duty, not lust for J.D., she shoved her feet into shoes, strode into the hallway, took the stairs downward two at a time and then went outside, bounding onto the long paved driveway.

The night was sultry and quiet, and when she strained her ears, she still didn't hear a car engine. Did that mean J.D. had arrived on foot? From where? He must be nearby, she decided. He would know that he couldn't get away with feigning his own death forever.

Or could he? Fear as well as other equally potent emotions she wasn't about to analyze, shot through her so she speeded her steps, then broke into a run. "J.D.?" she yelled, panting.

No answer.

Her breath quickening, she glanced behind her. The farther away she ran, the darker the house became. Trees surrounded her now, their leaves blocking the moonlight. Why hadn't she turned on the outside lights? Wait! There! To her right! Headlights winked through the trees!

So he'd driven after all! Through the foliage, she could see a car doing a U-turn on a nearby access road. It was heading back to Banner Manor. She watched it turn onto a red dirt path, which was a secondary way to get to the house.

Of course he'd come that way, she realized. If he'd risked approaching on the main driveway and parking in front of the house, somebody might have seen him. Intending to meet him halfway, she veered off the paved driveway, cut through the trees, and landed on the dirt path.

It was darker here thanks to a gauntlet of trees that banked the overgrown path. Overhead, thick, twisted branches stretched like long arms, meeting in the middle, obscuring stars. Leaves rustled in wind, and faraway, water rushed over rocks in the creek. Suddenly, she heard the soft chugging of the car's motor and glimpsed headlights again. Glancing toward the house, she saw a glimmer from the light in her and J.D.'s bedroom.

Then all the lights vanished.

The car was close now. Was he driving with the window down? Could he hear her? "J.D.?" she shouted.

She speeded her steps, her thighs straining, the muscles beginning to ache, her throat raw, burning from the sharp intake of air. There! Lights again! Then the motor cut off, the lights extinguished, and in the silence, she heard a door open and shut.

He was just ahead, standing under a shadowy copse. "It's just like you to run when we're not done talking!" she yelled.

His figure appeared in the road, jogging towards her. Raising her knees higher, she bolted in his direction. What if he'd decided to leave and never come back? What if he vanished, this time forever?

Not that she wanted him back, of course. And so, she had no idea what she'd say once he was in front of her, only that she was powerless but to chase him. If he disappeared again, only she would know he was alive! Only Mama Ambrosia would share the secret, and Mama had left town....

He was close now. Twenty yards...ten...five. Her heart stuttered. It wasn't J.D.! His steps were heavy, spaced too far apart. Too late, she tried to halt her own, but she was barreling toward him now, lunging on her own momentum. Thoughts crowded into her mind. Men were still dredging the river, searching for debris from the *Alabama*, looking for the definitive cause of the explosion. Could the person running toward her be involved in the recovery effort?

As they collided, he wrapped his arms around her. Screaming, she blinked in the pitch darkness, desperate to see as she twisted from his grasp. Then her heart flooded with relief. "Robby?" She gulped fast swallows of air. "Oh God…you scared me!"

"What are you doing out here? It's the middle of the night, Susannah, almost dawn!" Before she could answer, he disengaged himself, keeping a hand on her shoulder. "Like I told you earlier, I was going to check on you. I had to pull a near all-nighter and just got off work. I figured you understood that. When I saw you running toward me, I didn't know what to think. I—"

He must have taken the back road since it was the closest route from Lee Polls. "You scared me," she managed once more, barely able to catch her breath, her eyes darting to the trees. Her heart was beating dangerously hard, her words coming out fast. "I thought you were J.D. He was here, Robby. Right upstairs. In the bedroom. Just now. I swear I saw him. J.D.—he's alive! Someone else was on the boat!"

"No," Robby muttered in disbelief. He turned her toward the house, then grasped her hand. "C'mon," he murmured gently as he twined their fingers together. "We'd better get you inside."

She snatched away her hand. "You don't believe me?"

"Oh, Susannah," he whispered noncommittally.

"You've got to believe me! He was in our room!" Whirling, she bolted toward the main road. "I heard only one car motor," she called over her shoulder. "Yours. That means J.D.'s out here somewhere! Help me find him, Robby!" She raised her voice. "J.D.! Answer me!"

Lowering her voice, she asked, "Why did you tell me the body was J.D.'s, Robby? What proof did you and Sheriff Kemp have?"

Footsteps sounded behind her, then Robby's hand grabbed her shoulder once more. Forcibly turning her, he shook her lightly as if to bring her to her senses, but all she could think was that the arms didn't belong to J.D. Where Ellie might swoon, she felt nothing at this man's touch—no warmth, no passion, no need.

"Susannah," he said, "an attendant at the marina said J.D. was on board the *Alabama*. We found a man's remains. I don't know what just happened, but it looks like you've just had a bad dream. You've got to come inside now. J.D.'s gone. We spread his ashes to the four winds. Remember? You've got to accept this."

"No!" Panic filled her. Not even her best friends were going to believe her! What could she do? "And don't patronize me!"

"C'mon, sweetheart. Everybody's worried about you. When we get inside, I'm calling a doctor."

Robby was the one who was out of his mind! Did he really think she'd had some flight of fancy? Imagined something, the way her mama had sometimes? Just moments ago, J.D. had been in their bed again, lying on top of her, ready to make love. Now she wished they had! Emotions warred within her, tearing her apart. Her husband was gone, and no one would believe he was still alive! She loved him still…and sometimes, she hated him, too.

"He's out here!" she insisted. "In the trees, watching us." She raised her voice. "J.D.! Dammit, you've got to answer me! Make Robby believe me!"

Robby's grip tightened. "He's dead. I hate to be so blunt,

but it's for your own good. You have to get a hold of yourself, Susannah."

"You're wrong!"

"I wish I was."

"You're not listening because you don't care about him anymore."

He shook his head. "Not the way I used to. He changed, and we quit hanging out together, but I still consider him...a past best buddy."

She shook off his grasp once more and simply ran.

"Where are you going?" Robby shouted.

"To find my husband."

"I'M NOT LEAVING YOU later tonight," Ellie whispered the next evening in New York, leaning closer so Susannah could hear. "I promised Robby. I don't care what you say. He told me you were a mess last night, and I'm worried about you."

"Please understand," Susannah insisted, knowing how hard it had been for Ellie to talk at length with her ex. "I'm not up to attending any after-parties, but this is your chance to have a great time. You know, sleep with somebody other than Robby. Screw whatever he said to you about my mental health."

"He's concerned."

"I just...had a bad dream."

Susannah glanced toward her friend, but Ellie was busy taking in the crowded auditorium where the awards ceremony was being held. It was hard to believe that less than twenty hours earlier, Ellie's ex had been chasing Susannah around the grounds of Banner Manor. He'd finally dragged her inside and called a doctor, as he'd promised, who had tried to give her tranquilizers, which she'd just pretended to take. This morning, she'd caught the first flight to New York, only to land in a rainstorm that had continued all day.

As her plane had taken off this morning, she'd peered down at the tributaries and bayous receding below, half expecting J.D. to appear, but he hadn't. She shook her head, recalling how, the previous night, Robby had called Ellie, and for some time, they'd talked about Susannah's supposed near-breakdown.

Ellie squeezed her arm, her eyes narrowing. "Are you sure you're okay?"

"Am I going to crack up on stage if I have to accept the award for J.D., you mean?"

"I didn't say that."

"It's what you meant."

"Don't be mad. You know I can't stand it when we fight. I'm just worried. And I'm definitely going home with you after the ceremony."

"No," Susannah insisted. "I need to be alone." What if J.D. had followed her here? The man had attended his own funeral, so who knew? Maybe he'd have the nerve to attend his awards ceremony, too. "Really," she went on. "Go to all the parties, Ellie. It'll be fun. And while you're at it, convince people to make surprise appearances at my restaurant."

The idea seemed to appeal to Ellie's business sense. After all, she was an investor. "If I'd wanted to know any of these folks—" she glanced around the darkened auditorium once more "—I'd have hung around your house when they came to visit J.D."

"This is a different crowd," Susannah argued. "Mostly, anyway." Maureen, J.D.'s ex-publicist, had found Susannah and offered condolences that hadn't sounded particularly heartfelt. Worse, Susannah could swear she'd glimpsed Sandy, but then she'd vanished. Had J.D. told the truth about not having sex with her?

Would he appear again? He couldn't leave Susannah hanging like this! Someone else might have been killed in the accident on the *Alabama,* and Sheriff Kemp needed to be contacted. Someone had to do something!

But thanks to Robby, Susannah couldn't even tell Ellie what had happened. She was convinced that Susannah had been confused by a bad dream, then run outside, looking for J.D. Sheriff Kemp would be of no help, either, since she couldn't ask him to track a missing person he'd already pronounced dead. So Susannah was on her own.

"It would be a pity to waste that dress," Susannah ventured, coaxing Ellie so she could be alone. She didn't need a mama hen hovering over her tonight. Tomorrow she'd return to Banner Manor. Was J.D. there, maybe enjoying the house in her absence? Waiting for her return?

Susannah found herself surveying the crowd. All day she'd expected him to come around the corner, or walk through the door. Whenever a cell phone rang, she'd startle, sure he was calling. Even now, she felt his eyes on her back.

Realizing her hands were damp, she clasped them in her lap. Any moment, they would announce the award for which J.D. had been nominated. She might have to get up. The stage seemed impossibly far away, and from every direction, cameras were flashing, the bright lights blinding her so she wouldn't see him even if he were here.

In any case, he wouldn't show his face at a gathering of music industry professionals, would he? No...not even in disguise. She glanced at Ellie again, desperate to tell her the truth.

"Really," Susannah whispered again. "You have to go to at least one of the parties tonight. For my sake. I'll feel even worse if you don't." Fortunately, Ellie wanted to go. Who wouldn't? All around them were big names in the music industry, glamorous women wearing couture gowns and dazzling jewels, and rugged men in tuxedos, not all of them with dates.

"Are you sure you won't go with me?"

Relief filled Susannah. "No, but you go ahead. I'll wait for you at the apartment."

"Okay. But how can you think about parties right now? They're going to announce your category next."

"I only have to go up if J.D. wins."

"He will." Ellie paused. "But are you sure about the parties? I thought we might go to the restaurant. Maybe see Joe."

"And Tara?" Susannah shook her head. She'd promised Joe she'd stop by and she knew he was anxious to feel things were smoothed over between them, but not tonight. "I want to be alone. Do me a favor and go enjoy yourself tonight, though."

"It'll be good for you to get out."

"I don't want to."

"But you look amazing."

"Thanks." The dress wasn't as formal as those worn by some of the other women, but then, Susannah wasn't a singer. "J.D. bought the dress for me on one of his trips."

"When I imagined you inside this wrapper," J.D. had drawled, breezing through the door and handing her a box, "I only had one thought."

She'd laughed, opening the gift and tossing aside tissue paper. "Which was?"

"Taking that dress off you."

"I'll bet," she'd murmured, staring at the simple, calf-length garment. Swaths of criss-crossed champagne crepe fabric formed the bodice and a long matching shawl draped her shoulders, trailing to tattered ends that swirled around ballerina slippers studded with rhinestones.

Because his homecoming had degenerated into another fight, J.D. had never seen her in the dress. Tonight, she'd added diamonds—dangling earrings, a delicate bracelet and teardrop necklace. Suddenly, a voice drew her from her reverie, saying, "The nominees for CD of the year are…"

As the names were read, she held her breath, knowing J.D. was destined to win. His supposed passing had weighed in his favor, and while she resented what his craft had done to their marriage, she could admit his work deserved the prize.

Ellie's hand slid over hers as the announcer opened the envelope containing the winner's name. "Remember to smile," she whispered. "Win or lose, but I know he'll win." Ellie's voice caught. "I'm so sorry," she added in a quick whisper. "I wish he could be here for this, Susannah."

"Maybe he is. I mean, in spirit."

"And the winner is…" A drum roll sounded, and the announcer leaned nearer the microphone. "J. D. Johnson. For *Songs for Susannah.*"

Time seemed to stop. A melody from one of J.D.'s songs played. As J.D.'s voice filled the auditorium, her heart squeezed. He was singing about her—for her—the voice wickedly intimate. And yet, she had to be magnanimous and share that love with so many people she barely knew.

She could barely rise. So many people were watching! Tape from television cameras was whirring. The applause was thundering. Ellie gave her arm a final squeeze, and somehow she stood. Thoughts fled her mind. There was only the moment, and she was floating effortlessly toward the faraway stage. As she neared, the stairs looked daunting, her shoes, although flats, seemed dangerously unstable. What if she fell?

Before she knew it, she was traversing the stage, and a man was pressing a bronze statue into her hand. As her fingers curled around the cold metal, the applause died and she could have heard a pin drop. Staring into the sea of faces, she looked for J.D. but she could see only bright light. *This is what he sees when he sings,* she realized. No people, only shadows.

She had to say something! What choice did she have but to accept the award in good faith? It was hardly the right time to announce that J. D. Johnson was alive and well.

Besides, the audience, too, would think she was crazy. She imagined him calling out from the crowd, using this moment to surprise everyone, but he didn't. So she began her prepared speech.

"The work of so many people goes into making a CD that it would be hard to thank them all," she finally said. After a few more such comments, she concluded, "Everyone, from the artists who design the covers, to the technicians who mix the final sound, are completely necessary. My husband always knew that. If he were…"

She paused, barely able to lie. "If he were still alive," she forced herself to continue, feeling another burst of anger at J.D. for involving her in his dishonesty. "He would want me to thank every one of you. And you know who you are."

As J.D.'s music played again to thunderous applause, she silently cursed herself. Was she going to cover for J.D. forever? Furious as she was guided off the stage, she found herself back in her seat, clutching the statue, before realizing her ordeal wasn't over. J.D.'s music continued playing, in tandem with a montage of photographs of him projected onto a big screen. Then came the short interviews with musicians who spoke about the joy of playing with him. Casting a quick glance around the auditorium, she could see the emotion on the people's faces as they watched the tribute.

All at once, she felt overwhelmed—sad, wistful, angry

and yet somehow strangely selfish, too. She'd felt the same way at the funeral, since it was a reminder that J.D. was meant to be shared with the world, not just her. Had he been right last night? she suddenly wondered. Was she jealous? Afraid of his fame?

But no…she didn't feel jealous, exactly, just confused about the boundaries of their public and private lives. And now, seeing how many people had been positively affected by his music, she wished she'd tried harder. But would she, if given another chance? Unshed tears stung her eyes. Yes, she realized. He'd been right about her. Maybe she did fear his love for her wasn't strong enough to withstand fame and fortune….

Leaning toward Ellie, she whispered, "I'm going to cut out early."

Ellie looked concerned. "You have to stay, don't you?"

Promotional pictures had been taken at the beginning of the event, so Susannah shook her head. "No one will miss me. I did my duty. They'll understand." They'd believe her acceptance of the award had made her distraught about her husband's death. "I need to go back to the apartment."

"You're sure they won't miss us?"

She could hear the disappointment in Ellie's voice. "I'm going alone," Susannah said. When Ellie protested, Susannah shook her head. "I mean it. I just want to be by myself for a while, Ellie. It's been a big night."

Looking torn, Ellie frowned. "Are you sure you don't want company, Susannah?"

"Absolutely," she said.

But it was a lie. She wanted company all right—J.D.'s.

She wasn't sure what she'd say if she saw him again, but one thing was certain. He always made her body tingle, and she longed to feel his lips on hers again, if only for a goodbye kiss.

9

"HURRY!" From the back seat of the cab, J.D. peered through the windshield at the rain-streaked New York night as they got off the expressway. He was almost there! Good! The rhythmic thud of the wipers were like water torture as he closed his fingers around Sandy's bag. He'd taken it from Banner Manor days before, but he'd only looked inside a moment ago.

Now his stomach lurched as he visualized the contents— love letters addressed to him, written in a dark scrawl, along with defiled photographs of Susannah and a heart-shaped charm engraved with the words *I love you*. He'd given Susannah the pendant years ago, and presumably Sandy had stolen it. There were diary entries that even threatened Susannah's life…

"Can you try dispatch again?" he said.

"Don't worry. They called the cops. And we're almost there," he explained, his hawklike eyes assessing J.D. in the rearview mirror. "Are you sure your wife's in some kind of danger?"

"She could be."

"Like I said, dispatch called the cops."

Could Sandy be stalking Susannah? Holding Sandy's bag and his own duffel in his lap, he got ready to bolt from the cab. Silently he cursed himself for not rummaging through Sandy's things sooner, but why would he? He'd never given the woman a second thought. Besides, just thinking about her prompted bad memories.

"Damn," he whispered, remembering their arguments about his having so many near strangers in their house.

"You say something back there?"

"Just hurry."

"I'm trying." The man did a double-take. "You know, you look sort of like that guy…what's his name?"

J.D. managed a shrug. His own cheap cell phone wasn't getting a signal, and since it would have confused matters, he'd offered a false name when he'd asked the cabbie to call the police to Susannah and Ellie's Lower East Side address. Now J.D. was focused on getting there himself. He had no idea what he'd say when the cops got a good look at him, realized who he was and that he was alive.

"You know," the cabbie persisted, seemingly unfazed that they were heading toward a place where his passenger half expected trouble. "You look like that country-western singer who died a couple weeks ago. Did anybody ever tell you that?"

J.D. shook his head.

"His picture was in the papers. He got drunk and wrecked his boat or something." He paused. "Well, whatever his name was, you look like him. Not exactly. I think he might have been blond."

Here today, J.D. thought, gone tomorrow. He'd let his beard grow for the past few weeks, and he was wearing glasses and a baseball cap. Not much of a disguise, but he realized it didn't matter. People believed he was history. They certainly didn't expect to see him. Nobody looked too deeply, and nobody looked twice.

Realizing that, he suddenly wanted Susannah back more than ever. Their time together had meant something—it was

real. In the music world, everything was fleeting and imper-
sonal. His career had delivered the glamor it had promised,
but nothing J.D. had really craved.

And now Susannah could be in danger! It was his fault!

They'd just turned, and now the traffic was bumper to
bumper. He tried his cell again, but it still wasn't getting a
signal; the cabbie hadn't had a phone he could use. He'd have
called Robby at Lee Polls, too, and Sheriff Kemp. God only
knew what they'd say when they found out he was alive. Still,
things he'd found in Sandy's bag looked truly threatening….

Worse, J.D.'s gut said Sandy could be here. In New York.
Where Susannah was. If anything happened to her, J.D.'s resurrection from the grave would be the least of his problems.
He'd truly want to die if Susannah met any harm. As it turned
out Susannah had been right all along—while the other
woman had been in their house, she'd had her eyes on J.D.,
not Joel. That was why she'd stripped and slipped into bed
with him. She'd *wanted* Susannah to find them together.

His eyes darted to the sidewalks, scanning corners, looking
for pay phone or a police officer. Having the cab company's
dispatch operator call the police was all he could do. "I can't
believe this," he whispered, his mind conjuring a thousand
worst-case scenarios. Thankfully, they were almost at
Susannah's apartment.

"What?"

"Nothing," he muttered tersely, his fingers closing more
tightly around Sandy's bag, his stomach churning at what
he'd seen. Along with the rambling unsent love letters and
charm, there were some of his favorite pictures of him and
Susannah in bygone happier days. Susannah at the beach
wearing a pink bikini, her body wet, and another taken at a
picnic with her in shorts and a T-shirt. A silly lopsided,

devil-may-care grin had stretched her lips from ear to ear—it had been scratched out with a sharp object. One of Sandy's diary entries had read, "Only when I get rid of her can J.D. and I can be together. I know that's what J.D. secretly wants."

Hardly. After his fight with Susannah the other night, he'd gone to Mama Ambrosia's cabin. She'd said he could use it to, as she put it, "screw his head on straight" while she was on vacation. Then today, he'd decided to follow Susannah to New York. Until now, he'd forgotten about Sandy's bag. He hadn't felt right about tossing it. After all, maybe something valuable was inside….

He suppressed a shudder, replaying his conversation with Susannah the day the boat exploded. He'd been startled as he'd hung up the phone. Sandy had been standing there, silently watching and listening to him. How long had she been there? he'd wondered. When had she returned to Banner Manor? He hadn't seen her since he'd first asked her to leave months ago. As before, she'd apologized profusely, saying she'd wound up in his bed accidentally.

Now he knew it was a lie. Obviously she was crazy. And worse, crazy about him. He hadn't figured it out then. As always, his mind had been fixated on Susannah. Sandy claimed to have returned for some forgotten belongings, and although most of his friends had gone, J.D. had thought little of it. Maybe she'd come for the bag, but been unable to find it.

A chill raced down his spine.

"Oh, God," he whispered with dawning comprehension. The diary, photographs and stolen charm were disturbing, but the woman had known he was supposed to meet Susannah on the *Alabama*.

Had she blown up the boat? To kill Susannah? To get her

out of the way, so J.D. would love her instead? Was that why he'd run out of gas that night?

"I knew I had a full tank," he muttered softly.

For a second, it seemed improbable, but he was sure he was right. Maybe Sandy had siphoned off gas, so he'd be stranded and unharmed when the boat blew. But then who had died in the explosion?

Last night, as he lay on Mama Ambrosia's couch, his true predicament had really sunk in. Everybody thought he was dead, and Susannah, the one person he wanted to know the truth, had rejected him. He couldn't redeem himself in her eyes. He'd slept fitfully, waking only hours ago, knowing he had to see her again.

He'd called a private pilot he'd used in the past, sworn him to secrecy, and headed for New York, figuring he'd talk to Susannah after the awards ceremony. A car was supposed to meet them, and when it hadn't, he'd caught the cab.

But none of that mattered now. On the way downtown, he'd finally opened Sandy's bag. Of course, he'd barely noticed Sandy Smithers. He knew nothing about her—not her favorite color, or birthday, or where she was born—and yet…

"I let her in our house," he whispered. *Susannah's house*.

Once more, he thought of the photographs in the bag, the slashes across his wife's face. His thighs tensed, his fingers itched and he knew he couldn't wait. Maybe the subway would be faster. J.D. was sure Sandy was out there somewhere, and Susannah didn't even know she'd long been the object of another woman's hatred.

"Thanks," he suddenly said. "But I've got to get out." Leaning, he offered bills to the driver as he opened the door, stuffing Sandy's bag inside his own again so it would be easier to carry. What had been a small pink duffel only moments ago would soon become police evidence, he was sure of it.

Slinging his own bag over his shoulder, he thanked the cabbie once more, then ran headlong into the rain.

"THE LAST UMBRELLA," Susannah said with relief as she took out money, then heaved her oversize purse onto her shoulder, grunting with the weight, since J.D.'s award was inside. After paying the kiosk owner, she opened the inexpensive black umbrella. It wasn't very sturdy, but with luck, it would hold for a couple blocks until she reached her apartment.

"Or not," she muttered as a gust of wind threatened to turn the umbrella inside out. She pointed the tip downward like a spear so it wouldn't catch the wind again as she started jogging.

"Great," she groaned when the bronze statue started thumping her side. J.D. had already left her with enough bruises, emotional or otherwise, and the last thing she needed was this. The handbag had looked ridiculous with her fancy outfit, of course. Still, she'd have been lost without it, so she'd hidden it at her feet during the awards ceremony.

"What a life," she whispered, her mouth catching drops of rain. Everyone believed J.D. was dead, and now the prize for his work, one of the industry's most coveted honors, was stuffed into her purse like a worthless trinket. The moment defied anything she'd ever imagined. Weren't she and J.D. supposed to share this? Break out champagne? Make love?

Not that she was going to allow that to happen again, she vowed. She just wanted him to come clean so he wouldn't be deceiving so many people, and so that the authorities would start looking for the body of whomever had really been aboard the *Alabama* during the accident. She shook her head, shuddering as Robby's words from weeks ago replayed in her mind. *We think a faulty generator blew*.

"What a shame," she sighed, thinking of what a beautiful boat it had been. At least the explosion hadn't been J.D.'s fault. Still, she wished the real victim could be identified so they could be laid to rest. And where was J.D.

Mud splashed her hose as she landed in a puddle, and she groaned. A limo was to have picked her up after the ceremony, but because she'd cut out early, it hadn't been available, and she'd hailed a cab instead. Then the driver had missed a turn, and since he couldn't take her down her one-way street, she'd decided it was simpler to walk the rest of the way, despite the rain.

Speeding her steps, she felt relieved when Oh Susannah's came into view across the street. At the end of the block, she only had to turn a corner and she'd be able to see her and Ellie's front door. Not exactly home sweet home like Banner Manor, but the first floor, walk-up unit would be warm and dry.

Her teeth chattered in response to the chill that had come with the rain. After the trip down South, it felt as if the mercury was settling nearer to fifty degrees than sixty-five. At least Oh Susannah's was packed since the weather had driven people indoors.

Feeling drawn by the homey atmosphere—the lace curtains, country tablecloths and bright flowers in mason jars—she almost changed her mind about going to the apartment, but it was the wrong night to chat with Joe and Tara, so she kept running, rounding the corner. Besides, she'd visited the restaurant earlier today, to take care of business. And now she felt sure J.D. might materialize. He couldn't vanish….

Or could he? Maybe he was still at Bayou Banner. Here, the street was deserted, the windows dark in neighboring apartments. The Lower East Side had become more popular recently, but it wasn't as well trafficked as other downtown neighborhoods, and right now, it looked downright eerie.

Suddenly, her heart started hammering, and for no reason she could fathom, she stopped in her tracks. Turning to peer over her shoulder, she instinctively grabbed her purse, either to protect J.D.'s award or to use it as a weapon—she wasn't sure which.

But no one was there.

Her eyes scanned the street. Who had she expected to see? J.D.? She tried to push aside the foreboding that had plagued her all night, but she couldn't. She felt as if someone were following her…watching her.

"It's just the rain," she whispered nonsensically, mostly to hear her own voice. Reaching into her purse as she mounted the steps to her building, she dug inside for the key. As she inserted it into the lock, her hand quivered. God, she felt unsettled!

She wrenched around. She'd had the same spooked feeling at Banner Manor. Countless times, late at night, she'd go to the windows, believing people were outside, watching the house.

"And it was J.D.," she reminded herself as she opened the door onto the foyer. She tried to catch her purse, but it slid from her shoulder. Letting it fall to the floor, she used it as a doorstop for the outer door while she shook excess rain from the umbrella. Relief flooded her as she stepped from the stoop into the hallway. Finally she was home. Since the door to the apartment was within reach, she simultaneously opened it as she set the umbrella aside, then reached back for her handbag.

While the apartment door was swinging inward, she realized the answering machine was playing. Drats. She'd never make it to the phone.

Robby's voice filled the apartment. "Sheriff Kemp and I have been trying to track you down for hours, Susannah. We tried the awards ceremony, but they said you couldn't be disturbed. It's about the boat. I don't know if you got my other messages. We found something…and well, you need to call me as soon as possible. The explosion…it wasn't an accident, as it turns out. We thought it was the result of a faulty generator, but now we think there might be foul play."

She started to dart into the apartment to grab the phone, but she didn't want to leave the outer door open for strangers. Tilting her head, she remained quiet to listen to the rest of Bobby's message.

"And, Susannah?" he added. "I think you should get out of there. Ellie, too."

Then the line went dead. She quickly snatched her purse from the floor. She sensed there was more to the story, but he'd said enough. Something was wrong. Did it have to do with J.D.'s reappearance? She'd have to call Robby back right away. Swiftly, she reached to shut the outer door, but as she did, she heard a *pa-ching*.

Something sprayed her stockings! Her eyes darted downward. Splinters? Yes, wood had been gouged from the door frame, inches from her leg.

"What?" She turned to get a better look. Just then, something slammed her hard from behind, knocking the wind from her, sending her sailing toward the open apartment door.

Everything went black.

She heard the outer door slam shut, then she felt herself being half dragged into the apartment.

She tried to scramble away, reaching for the statue to use as a weapon as she made her way behind the sofa. Her mind raced. What was going on?

Blinking against the darkness, her heart pounding, she watched a bulky shadow lunge to the window and lift the curtain's edge, then the shadow ducked. She heard a soft clink before the glass shattered. Something hit the wall behind her. *Pa-ching. Pa-ching. Pa-ching.*

Are those bullets? Oh my God!

The man dove, hauling what looked to be a large bag. With his free hand, he yanked her to her feet. "Is there another way out?"

"J.D.?"

"We have to be quiet. We have to get out of here. Now."

She bolted wordlessly toward a bedroom fire door that led to a back staircase and the basement of the building. Moments later, they'd cut through a laundry room, emerging in a back alley.

Tightly, he grasped her hand, twining his fingers through hers. Even now, under the circumstances, she couldn't help but feel a shiver of longing at the touch. She felt the dry skin and strength of his muscles, the perfect fit of the hand against her palm. Despite the hatred she kept professing to have for him and whatever danger they were in, her heart was soaring, since he'd returned. But just as quickly, annoyance rushed in.

"Robby called just now," she said as they ran. Her shoes were thin, and the pavement was cold, strewn with debris, and it slowed her down.

"What's making that noise?" he whispered, glancing at her bag. His voice was steady although she was starting to feel winded.

"Your award," she whispered.

"Lose it," he urged. "Just toss it."

She couldn't, it was irreplaceable. She held onto it, her breath shallow with exertion, her lungs burning as the apartment receded behind them. One block, two…she counted. Three…

Suddenly, she gasped, doubling and grasping her side. "I can't run in these shoes anymore, J.D."

Tugging her arm, he pulled her behind some trash cans, and she squatted, the hem of the beautiful dress he'd given her soaking up mud. He craned his neck, scanning the alley, and the longer she took in his profile, the harder it was to hate him. His eyes were alert, almost predatory, his body tense and impossibly still. Power coiled inside him and he looked ready to pounce. Just looking at him made her feel safe.

"Were those gunshots?" she gasped, gulping air, already knowing the answer. A girl didn't grow up in Mississippi without knowing how a gunshot sounded.

"I think so."

Something had definitely gouged the door frame and shattered the window. "What on earth's going on?"

"It's a long story."

"You know why somebody just shot at me?" It was just like J.D. to be cryptic. Annoyance flared. "Dammit, J.D., if somebody's shooting at me, and you know why, I have a right to know, too!"

"Not here."

"I'm not going a step farther until I get some answers." Even if it meant she had to crouch behind smelly garbage and what was probably a safe haven for city rodents. She added, "Robby just called saying the explosion on the boat wasn't an accident."

J.D. turned toward her, and as his gaze trailed from the top of her head to the tips of her toes, she felt a rush of unbidden sensual burning heat. As much as she wanted to ignore the sensation, she was being quickly reminded why she'd married the man. He wasn't winded, but his chest expanded and fell with deep breaths, making his pectorals look infinitely touchable.

He exhaled a heartfelt curse when his eyes landed on her feet. "You're practically barefoot."

Once more he was blaming her for something that was really his fault, and she felt another rush of pique. "You're the one who bought me the shoes."

"Yeah," he said simply.

Suddenly, everything was too much. She was in some sort of danger she didn't understand. Drenched. And wearing a see-through dress to boot. Without looking, she knew the eye makeup she'd worn for the ceremony had melted down her cheeks. Her stockings were dirty and shot through with runs, and J.D. was exactly right. She *was* practically barefoot. No longer warm from running, the night air caused her to shiver.

"I didn't exactly anticipate running in this weather?" she huffed. "I mean, it's not like I want to catch my death out here, J.D." Pausing, she acerbically added, "Not everybody is as happy as you to go to their grave, you know."

Wordlessly he rummaged in his pocket and withdrew a handkerchief, swiping it beneath her eyes. Sure enough, her mascara had run. And leave it to J.D., she thought with escalating fury, to remind her that he was the only man she knew who actually still carried handkerchiefs. He might forego underwear with frightening regularity, but he always had a hanky handy for the ladies.

Now he brushed away a damp lock of hair that had fallen into her eyes, and his gaze softened, as if he was relieved to see she was fine. "C'mon," he said, standing.

"Whither thou goest, I will go?" she guessed as she stood, too. "Isn't that a bit demanding for a guy who's supposed to have passed onto a better life?"

They were toe to toe, and rocking back on her bare heels, she surveyed him. Only her fury at J.D. could override her sense of self-protection and worry over what had just happened at her apartment. "And is it really a better life?" she continued, feigning real interest. "I mean, pardon me for asking, but I've never had the opportunity to interview somebody who's just come back from the other side. What do they have there? Pearly gates? Harps for all your musician friends?"

Puffing his cheeks, he stared at her a long moment, his searing blue eyes narrowed and his lips pursed tightly, as if it was costing him not to offer snide retorts. He could, too, she knew—J.D. had a way with words. He gave her a pointed look, as if to ask if she were done with her tirade. Then, silently, he re-shouldered his duffel. Before she could protest, he leaned agilely, hooked an arm under her knees and simply scooped her into his embrace—handbag and all.

The next thing she knew, he was cradling her against his chest. She told herself that she had no choice but to wreathe her arms around his neck, but as she did so, she was assaulted with pine and peppermints, a combination of scents that was pure J. D. Johnson. Or almost. She sniffed. "For once, I don't smell whisky," she commented.

"Told you," he muttered. "I'm on the wagon."

"Better than on your boat, apparently. And what do you think you're doing?" she said with pique, trying to ignore a traitorous beating of her heart against his.

"Carrying you."

"Hmm. Well, if you think we're going to get more physical than this, you're dead wrong."

"Fine by me."

She doubted that. "Am I allowed to know where we're going?"

"To find Ellie." He paused. "And then home to Banner Manor. A plane's waiting at the airport."

"Flown by whom?"

"A pilot I know."

"Aren't you afraid he'll tell the world you're alive, well and having a great time?"

J.D. was actually starting to look rattled. So much so that she was beginning to enjoy herself. "Nope."

"And why's that?"

"Because I'm not having a great time right now, Susannah."

"That makes two of us. Now, what about my place?"

"Before I got there, I called the cops. They're on their way."

Sure enough, she could hear sirens. Of course, in New York, that wasn't unusual. Her heart beat double time as the long strides of J.D.'s jeans-clad legs continued swallowing the pavement. Somehow, she wasn't surprised to find her husband could manage both her weight and his duffels without stumbling, but she still had no idea what was happening.

"Were those really gunshots?" she asked again, realizing the shock of the past few moments was starting to subside. "Why did you suspect something was wrong? How did you know to call the police?"

His face drew her eyes like a magnet, and she couldn't help but stare up at him, registering the heady scent of his breath. She watched as his jaw clenched, making enticing shadows flicker over his cheeks in the darkness. Finally he said, "Remember Sandy Smithers?"

She stiffened in his arms, and everything inside her turned to ice. "The gorgeous naked woman who was in bed with you? How could I forget?"

"I think she got into bed with me on purpose that morning," he said, releasing a worried sigh as they reached a main avenue. He seemed to be looking for a cab.

"No kidding," she returned angrily, wiggling against him. Moments ago, she'd been kept warm by the exertion of running and then from his body heat, but now, she'd rather brave the dirt and mud of the streets than continue to let him held her. "Look," she muttered, squirming. "Why don't you put me down?"

He did so, then watched as she crossed her arms over her chest. Catching his gaze, she realized once more how wet she was, and how the delicate fabric of the dress had become nearly transparent. Her arms had just served to lift her breasts, as if offering them for his perusal.

"I'm not going anywhere with you until you tell me what's going on," she stated firmly, trying to ignore the heat and hunger flaring in his eyes.

"I think she's stalking you, Susannah," he said simply.

She gasped. "Who? Sandy Smithers?"

"Yeah." He nodded. "I think she may have just shot at you." He paused. "And me. And I think she blew up the *Alabama*."

It was the last thing she'd expected him to say. Her lips parted in shock. "Why would she do that?"

For the first time in her recollection, J.D. actually looked scared. "Because she thought you were the person on board, Susannah."

10

BECAUSE SHERIFF KEMP WAS a massive man, his tan uniform nearly burst the shoulder seams as he hunched to scrutinize the contents of Sandy's bag, which were laid out on his desk. He'd been called away from a date with Delia, and at first, when he'd seen J.D., he'd been shocked. Then he'd quickly begun questioning him about the explosion.

Now, when he glanced up, his brown eyes, visible through blond bangs, held less judgment than J.D. knew he deserved. That made him feel guiltier, if it was possible, and as self-loathing filled him, he damned himself for all the trouble he'd caused. He was beginning to wish the earth would open and swallow him, and since that's what so many people thought had happened to him, a bemused smile tugged his lips—only to disappear when he thought of the danger in which he'd put Susannah.

"Well," said the sheriff, "do we tell the media you're alive?"

J.D. shrugged, ready to ignore anything that didn't pertain to Susannah's safety. Not that he could. Robby had shown up to help, and if it weren't for the circumstances, it would seem like old times. Robby was leaning against a wall, an inscrutably furious scowl on his face, almost like the one he'd worn throughout his hardscrabble childhood, during which his mama was gone and his daddy was drinking all the time.

Displaying his usual attitude of defiance, Robby's hands were shoved angrily into the slacks pockets of one of the fancy suits he always wore to work, and he looked gaunt and harried, like the workaholic he'd become. His chestnut hair was shaggy, as if he'd been too busy to visit a barber, and it nearly obscured his glittering eyes, but not enough to hide his emotions. Astonishment was warring with betrayal, then something that might have been pleasure that J.D. wasn't really dead, but Robby was trying to hide the latter.

Susannah had claimed the room's only armchair, and she was wearing white tube socks, compliments of the sheriff, along with her ruined dress. Her shoes were drying in a windowsill. A gray wool army blanket was slung around her shoulders, looking incongruous with a diamond necklace and dangling earrings. Unfortunately, there had been no clothes for them to change into on the plane, so Susannah had just toweled herself dry. Now J.D. felt a surge at his groin as he recalled how good she'd looked, slowly dabbing her bare, shapely, mud-streaked legs after she'd stripped off the ruined panty hose.

The woman he'd feared he'd never hold again had felt great in his arms, too, even if he'd been cuddling her against her will. He pushed his thought aside. This was no time to have sex on the brain; then again, that was a tall order when Susannah was around.

At least for him. His estranged wife was studying everything in Sheriff Kemp's office, from the gunmetal-gray desks to the gleaming white tile floor to the area maps that adorned the walls. *Anything but me,* J.D. realized ruefully.

An unwanted memory assaulted him of the day he'd first seen the dress she was wearing. It was in the window of a dressmaker's shop. Maybe it was the sensual skirt, made of airy, multilayered fabric, or the unusual tattered hem, but whatever the case, the champagne-colored garment had stopped him in his tracks, and he'd known it was tailor-made for Susannah's statuesque figure, nipped waist and full breasts.

"She'd look gorgeous in it," he'd whispered.

And she had. Although he'd never seen her wear it until tonight, and their run through the rain had destroyed it. How was he going to forgive himself if something happened to her? He'd give his life to save Susannah. If Sandy Smithers had really destroyed the *Alabama* and tried to kill Susannah, what would the woman do next?

Thoughtfully, J.D. chewed the inside of his cheek, then stopped when his gaze landed on the sheriff's desk. *Amazing,* he thought. One of the most coveted awards known to the music industry was propped there, next to Susannah's oversize purse. The award meant nothing now. A chintzy hunk of gold not worth the pain it had brought into his and Susannah's lives. J.D. wished he'd never learned to play music. To hell with the hours of pleasure it had brought him.

Shaking his head, he made a silent vow to himself. *If Susannah doesn't get hurt,* he thought, *I swear I'll never play again.*

"Uh...J.D.?"

Glancing up, he realized the sheriff was speaking to him. In fact, everybody was staring at him. He was so preoccupied that he hadn't paid any attention to the conversation. "We do whatever you think is best," he said to the sheriff. "I'll play this any way you want." *Anything, if Susannah is safe. Please.* The closest thing he'd ever felt to humility filled his soul. *Don't let my mistakes hurt my wife.*

"Glad to hear it." Sheriff Kemp nodded abruptly and feathered a splayed hand through his blond curls. Then he used the eraser end of a pencil to prod the items on the desk again. They made J.D. shudder, especially the destroyed pictures of Susannah.

"We'll send these to the lab," Sheriff Kemp said, thoughtfully turning the pages of a diary decorated with childish hearts and cupid's arrows. Words on the pages flew by: *Sandy loves J.D. Sandy and J.D. forever. Sandy wants J.D.'s babies.* Toward the back of the book, the woman's scrawl became less legible; she'd been pressing the pen point harder, causing tiny tears in the paper, and she'd become more obsessed with Susannah. *Why can't J.D. see through her? Doesn't he know she's a big fake? Why doesn't he leave her?*

And later: *Somebody has to save J.D. by showing him the truth. He's too nice to see through that bitch. She doesn't love him. She's just using him for his money and fame. I wish she'd die.*

"We'll look carefully where you kept your truck parked that night," Sheriff Kemp continued, "and where we found it the night of the explosion.

"Gas might have soaked into the ground near the road, but it's rained since then." The sheriff nodded distractedly. "We'll check though."

"When the truck stopped running, I guided it under some trees," J.D. said helpfully.

"There was no need to examine the area before, but if Sandy Smithers is responsible for the events tonight, or if she's the reason you never reached the *Alabama* so you wouldn't be onboard when it blew, then maybe we'll find evidence."

"And the truck itself?" asked Robby, studying the photographs where Susannah's face had been defiled. "Maybe there's a compromised fuel line. We had towed it to the garage," he continued. "It's been there for the past two weeks.

The owner said we could keep it there until the estate gave word about what to do with it."

"Any idea where this woman might have gone?" the sheriff asked.

"None," said J.D., "but my gut says she's the one who shot at us in New York. Maybe she's still there."

"Or maybe she followed you here." Robby's voice was a low rumble akin to a growl. Clearly he was none too happy about Ellie possibly being in danger.

Sheriff Kemp kept on point, addressing J.D. "Did the shooter see you?"

J.D. shrugged as the sheriff started taking notes. "I figure. I headed to the awards ceremony from the airport, but when I saw the contents of the bag, I changed directions. If my hunch was right, and Sandy was in town, I knew I'd be better off going to the apartment to make sure Susannah was safe. I didn't think Sandy wouldn't try to hurt her at the ceremony. There's just too much security."

"Don't talk about me as if I'm not here, J.D.," Susannah said.

He could do nothing right at the moment. Taking a deep breath, he said, "Sorry, Susannah." Then he continued, "Because of the rain, I waited a couple doors down from Ellie and Susannah's, under an awning. Susannah came home from the other direction, so I didn't see her at first. It was dark and an umbrella was covering her face. She was nearly inside before I realized it was her."

Pausing, he shook his head, trying to remember. "I saw a flash from my left from behind a parked car, just as Susannah got the key in the door. It was just a bolt of light, and I heard a gunshot."

Sheriff Kemp was listening hard. "And then?"

"I ran toward Susannah." He hadn't thought, only acted. "I hopped a rail, ran up some stairs and pushed her inside."

"But you didn't see the shooter?"

"No."

"But the shooter probably saw you."

J.D. nodded. "Yeah. I guess. I mean, the porch light was on when I ran inside."

"Was it still raining?"

"Yeah. Hard."

With the pencil, the sheriff nudged a photograph on his desk. It was a five-by-eight of Susannah in the prom dress J.D. had so carefully removed before making love to her the night they'd eloped. The picture had been stabbed repeatedly, maybe as many as thirty times. "A knife or scissors," the sheriff said absent mindedly.

Susannah gasped. "I knew pictures were missing. While I was cleaning the house after…" She paused. "After J.D.'s funeral." She shook her head. "Most of those were in an album near the downstairs TV, but that one was in a frame upstairs."

"Susannah's face has either been scratched or cut out of ten pictures, at least," J.D. said, anxiety gnawing at him. "How dangerous do you think Sandy is?"

Sheriff Kemp shook his head. "We don't even know she's connected to the explosion. All you've got is proof she's obsessive and has a violent imagination." Sheriff Kemp glanced toward the door to the evidence room. "However, we now have proof explosives were onboard the *Alabama*. That's why Robby was trying desperately to reach Susannah. Unfortunately, they didn't speak before you two were shot at. Still, that doesn't mean Sandy Smithers is the perpetrator."

Surprisingly, when she spoke again, Susannah's voice was rock steady, and maybe, J.D. thought, that was the worst thing. It was as if she'd prepared for this long ago. Obviously, she thought such trouble was a natural consequence of loving J. D. Johnson.

"What's going on in New York?" she asked.

Sheriff Kemp shrugged. "When you two arrived, I was just hanging up with the NYPD. They closed shop at your apartment. Some bullets hit the door frame, and they found footprints. Heavy boots, maybe military, small size."

"Sandy usually wore boots," J.D. offered. "She was pretty, but—"

Susannah snorted. "Try gorgeous."

"But she didn't dress in a feminine way," J.D. finished.

"Too bad they didn't find something more personal," Susannah offered dryly. "Panties. A bra, maybe. Then J.D. could really help."

She was testing his patience. While he didn't expect Susannah to support him after all his mistakes, he'd never slept around. "Let's keep it private, Susannah."

"That's rich coming from you."

At the sheriff's heavy sigh, she pursed her lips. He said, "And there's nothing else of hers at Banner Manor?"

Susannah shook her head. "While I was cleaning, I never saw anything I didn't recognize."

"What about the bag?"

"I never noticed it. J.D. said it was half buried under some of his stuff. I'd started cleaning upstairs and in the living room. I was..."

"Distraught?" suggested the sheriff.

"However unnecessarily," Susannah conceded.

They all fell silent.

"Well," the sheriff continued. "Like I said when you first got here, you heard bullets, all right. As it turns out, they're from a twenty-two revolver."

"Not much of a weapon," commented Robby.

Susannah gasped. "What about your gun, J.D.?"

"Oh no," he whispered. Years ago, he and Robby used to target shoot with a twenty-two all the time, knocking soda cans off hay bales. He hadn't used it for years, another reminder of his estrangement from Robby. "I take it out once a year and clean it," he stated. "It was in the back of the bedroom closet, on a top shelf."

"I didn't touch anything there," Susannah said.

"She took your gun," Robby muttered.

"Registered?" asked the sheriff.

"Sure," J.D. said. "It was a gift from my dad."

Sheriff Kemp sighed as if to say it was going to be a long night. "An officer told me Ellie will be staying with a fellow named Joe O'Grady. I don't think she's in any danger, but it's a necessary precaution." Sheriff Kemp glanced at Susannah. "Do you know him?"

"Uh…yeah." And then as if simply to cause J.D. pain, she added, "Pretty well, actually."

"Then he'll take care of her," the sheriff said with a nod.

"That's crazy!" Robby bellowed, looking furious. "I'm going to New York."

"I don't think you should," Susannah put in quickly.

It had been so many years since they'd all gotten along, J.D. thought sadly. He and Robby used to fish the bayous, using bait from his dad's shop, while Susannah and Ellie watched, sunning themselves in bikinis on a blanket. Or they'd jam on drums and a guitar, while Susannah and Ellie danced.

Withdrawing his hands from his pockets, Robby crossed his arms. "Ellie could be in danger, too. She could have been with you tonight."

"She'll be fine with Joe," Susannah assured him. "He's

got a new girlfriend, by the way," she added to smooth his ruffled feathers. "And don't forget, Robby, this woman hates me, not Ellie."

"I'm going," Robby said resolutely.

"I think we ought to do whatever the sheriff thinks best," J.D. offered.

Robby sent him a look that was full of fire but still chilled J.D.'s blood. "You've caused enough trouble," Robby warned. "I came here for Susannah and Ellie, not you."

A long silence fell; it was more than J.D. could take. He wanted to argue, fight back and protest, but Robby was right. He hadn't deserved such good friendships. Not with Robby and Ellie, and least of all, with Susannah.

"What about my restaurant?"

J.D. could almost see Susannah's mind working. Would Sandy Smithers sabotage the eatery? Destroy it the way she had the *Alabama*? At the same time, was Sandy even the culprit? Had J.D. shut his mind to the possibility that someone else was responsible as the sheriff kept implying? Maybe, J.D. admitted. After all, he wanted to know the identity of the enemy immediately. It made what was happening seem more manageable. More contained. And it made fighting back easier.

"I need to keep these items as evidence, of course," the sheriff remarked.

J.D. nodded.

Sheriff Kemp shook his head. "For whatever it's worth, I do figure you're right. This woman may well have let the gas out of your truck so you couldn't meet Susannah. She didn't know Susannah wasn't coming. After the explosion, maybe she thought she'd killed you accidentally. She must have hated herself. Then…"

"She saw him." Susannah inhaled audibly, her eyes widening. J.D. watched as her hand flew to her neck. As she did when she was anxious, she touched the charm she wore around her neck; Ellie had one just like it.

Running the charm up and down on its chain, Susannah said, "Maybe Sandy's been watching the house all along. I felt someone outside the whole time I was there. Later, I thought it was J.D. But maybe, when he came back, she was out there, too, and she saw him."

"She could have felt even more betrayed that he'd survived," the sheriff agreed. "Or that J.D. was more duped by Susannah than ever."

"Then she started to target me again," Susannah posited.

Sheriff Kemp shook his head. "We'll find out. In the meantime, you and Ellie are safe. We'll run a background check to see if this woman had reason to know anything about explosives."

"She never said anything about them," J.D. mentioned, still watching Susannah toy with her necklace, the creamy column of her neck completely captivating. "I would have remembered something like that. She didn't say anything about guns, either."

The sheriff nodded. "Do you mind if I look around the house?"

Susannah shook her head. "I can walk you through."

"Not yet. Tonight you two can't go back to Banner Manor," the sheriff returned. "Better safe than sorry." He looked at J.D. "And there's no need to muddy up the waters by announcing you're alive. Let's hold that card close to the vest, in case we need it."

"Whatever you want," returned J.D. "The only other person who knows is the pilot who brought us here. For a minute, I thought a cabbie in New York recognized me, but he didn't. Oh," he added, "Mama Ambrosia. She knows, but she won't say anything. She offered me her cabin while she's out of town."

"Excellent." The sheriff nodded, looking relieved. "You and Susannah can stay there."

"What!" Susannah exploded. "With him? No offense, but you're as crazy as Sandy Smithers. I'd rather run the risk of being shot at again."

"I don't have the manpower to protect you," the sheriff returned calmly.

"I'd offer," Robby said, giving J.D. a long glance of censure, "but I'm going to New York to make sure Ellie's safe."

"I don't know how she'll react to that," Susannah said gently.

"I'm going anyway," Robby said.

"I'll go to Hodges' Motor Lodge," Susannah vowed.

J.D.'s heart was sinking. "I know how you feel about me, Susannah. Robby, too. That's a given. But the sheriff's right. He doesn't have manpower, and you'll be safer at Mama's. I'll keep to myself. Even if Sandy's heard of Mama Ambrosia, she couldn't know the location. The cabin's tucked in the woods. Half the time, even locals can't find it."

"No way am I going to some fortune-teller's house," Susannah protested, still worrying her charm.

J.D. was about to respond, but his blood quickened, and before he thought it through, he was striding across the room. His hand closed over the chain, and something inside him softened when he felt the warmth of Susannah's hand. "What's this?" he asked, voice strangely hoarse.

"My chain." Susannah suddenly gasped. "The other chain…the one the sheriff gave me after the *Alabama* blew. He said they found it in the wreckage. It's a Saint Christopher's medal, and I'd never seen it before, but I thought you might have gotten it recently. The sheriff thought it was yours, and in a state of shock…"

"Oh, dammit. I'm so sorry," Sheriff Kemp suddenly interjected. "There's no excuse for the shoddy work we did. It was incompetent, but we'll correct that now. I'm not asking you two to forgive me. You know we never get crime like this around here, and the media was pressuring us. Besides which, we all knew J.D. personally, and that public relations lady from New York was harping all the time. If the truth be told, I'd been thinking of nothing but Delia all the time, anyway. Everything happened so fast…

"And we were so sure it was J.D. We'll question the attendant again, but he said he'd left the marina to pick up some for dinner, and when he returned, he saw the boat on the water with J.D. in it."

"I called and told him to have it ready," J.D. said. "He must have just assumed it was me."

"We'll talk to him again." Sheriff Kemp blew out a sigh. "He told us that you've never let anybody else play captain, either."

"No," J.D. said abruptly, "I didn't." He was still staring at the Saint Christopher's medal that rested against his palm. He thought it was supposed to ensure safety, but this time around, it hadn't.

"You did a fine job," she assured the sheriff.

"Given what you knew, it seemed the person onboard had to be me," J.D. agreed. "But I think it was a guy named Joel Murray."

Susannah glanced up at him. "Joel?"

"He was a studio musician without any family," J.D. explained to the sheriff. "He travels to play with different bands. He's not much of a concert musician. Anyway, the record company sent him here to work with me. He brought Sandy, but she wasn't nearly as interested in him as he was in her."

Somehow J.D. pulled his gaze from Susannah's eyes. He glanced over his shoulder at the sheriff who said, "Why do you think Joel Murray was onboard?"

"Because he always wore a Saint Christopher's medal," J.D. said. "And he wore it on a strip of leather, not a chain, just like this."

11

AT MAMA AMBROSIA'S, Susannah rubbed a patch of condensation from the bathroom mirror and peered at her reflection. "Passable," she decided, then mentally berated herself for caring about her appearance at such a time. Still, how could she help but feel vain when J.D. practically salivated every time he looked at her?

Mama's cabin was far more inviting at second glance. The main room Susannah had visited previously wasn't much to look at, mostly due to the utilitarian shelves lined with potions and herbs and an antique potbelly stove, but farther down a hallway, toward a back door that opened onto a porch with a rocking chair, were three cozy bedrooms, all laid with wide-planked floors and paneled with hardwoods. The curtains were clean and white and the beds made with crisp sheets and pastel quilts.

"I'll take this room," J.D. had said, nodding toward the smallest as Susannah headed for the shower. "It's the one I was staying in before."

"Are you sure Mama isn't going to mind?"

"She offered me her cabin while she's gone."

Susannah suspected Mama had been matchmaking, not that the ideas she'd planted were going to bear fruit. "Are you sure you don't want to sleep outside?" Susannah had continued sweetly, as if to say J.D. should seriously consider it. She'd expected some testy retort; maybe she'd even been trying to rile him intentionally, to take the edge off the fact that they weren't exactly in spacious Banner Manor, but alone in a cabin the size of a postage stamp. He merely nodded, not rising to the bait. "You could be out there with your friends, the animals," she'd added.

A beat passed, then he'd simply said, "I'll fix some food, Susannah. I figure you're hungry."

"I'll just take a shower," she'd huffed, turning on her heel and heading inside the bathroom, hardly wanting to examine her pique. Surely she was spoiling for a fight just to make sure she kept J.D. at a distance, not because she wanted to get into a heated discussion with the man.

Still, she was starting to feel sorry for him. Clearly bothered by Sandy and by Robby's cold reception, J.D. had kept silent on the way to the cabin. Sheriff Kemp had followed Robby to Banner Manor to get Susannah's car, then they'd picked up food supplies at a store halfway to Bayou Blair. Robby had brought her a pair of flip-flops and a bag of clothes from the same store, mostly sweatpants with logos from sports teams Susannah didn't recognize. She'd rather have had things from her own house, but Sheriff Kemp didn't want her to return there until he was sure she'd be safe.

After she finished dressing in a white T-shirt and gold drawstring pants and a matching hoodie, she took a deep breath and headed toward the kitchen, her throat suddenly aching when she recalled the disdain with which Robby had treated J.D. It was so sad. Worse, Robby would blame J.D. further if something happened to Ellie.

Pushing aside thoughts of the gunshots that could have taken their lives, Susannah walked toward the scent of seasoned meat. Pausing in the doorway, she waited to see if J.D. would turn around, but he continued lifting lids on pots and stirring the contents. "Is that you?"

"No, it's Sandy Smithers."

"Not funny."

He was right, it wasn't. It was easy to stare at his back, though, especially since he'd taken off his shirt. He had nice broad shoulders and pronounced shoulder blades, a back strong enough to make any woman shiver, with myriad ridges and sloping contours, not to mention invitingly smooth skin. As Susannah's eyes settled on his behind, her fingers itched. Unbidden, her gaze settled hotly just above the thick, hand-tooled belt he wore with his jeans.

"What's cooking?" Despite the fact that the food smelled heavenly, she added, "Did you season with spices from those jars down the hallway?"

"I would have, but I couldn't find any herbs that would make our problems go away."

"Which ones?"

"Any of them." He shot an apologetic glance over a bare shoulder as he transferred steaks to the plates. For the briefest second, when she saw his eyes, thoughts of Sandy Smithers ceased to exist. A man hadn't been killed. The world didn't think J.D. had passed on, and the two of them hadn't run for their lives through the streets of New York. Just looking at J.D. had always made her feel safe. Which was ridiculous, since he was the most dangerous and annoying man she'd ever known.

As she surveyed the steaks, Susannah was suddenly aware of her rumbling stomach and watering mouth. Now it was she, not J.D., who was salivating. She felt a surge of relief, too, since the object of her emotions was a sirloin, not her almost-naked nearly ex-husband.

At least until he turned fully around, a plate in each hand, and her throat turned as dry as dust. Maybe it was the smoothness of the skin, the wealth of wild black tangled chest hair, the muscular pectorals or the nipples that looked just a tad too taut. Whatever it was, her body was responding, her chest filling like a sail on a sudden intake of breath, then growing tight when she inadvertently held it.

Then the moment passed. He'd set napkins and cutlery on the center island, and she sidled closer, seating herself on a tall stool, just as he did. She eyed him as he set her food before her, then she dug in, cutting a healthy bite from the meat. "It looks good," she conceded. "Even worse, it tastes divine."

"You don't want to like it?"

"No more than I want to like you."

"I don't blame you."

Damn, she thought, feeling strangely miffed again. "It's not like you to be so agreeable."

He shot her a look. "I can't even do that right."

Warm and succulent, the meat was as good as a juicy kiss, and her tummy melted as she swallowed. Before she thought it through, she added between her next bites, "You always were a good cook."

He was eating just as fast as she, as if starved. "When I bothered to do it, anyway."

She let that pass, but as she silently devoured the best meal she'd had in awhile, at least outside her own restaurant, she felt further unsettled. Guilty even. Oh, J.D. had gotten too full of himself. In fact, for the past couple years, he'd morphed into the incarnation of every bad male quality known to womankind—rolled into one hunky package. And he never should have let so many strangers crash land into their lives. Definitely, he shouldn't have made a split-second decision to let the world think he was dead.

But he couldn't have known Sandy was crazy. While tonight's events were hardly a blessing in disguise, over the past weeks—from the day Susannah had thought J.D. was gone forever—she'd been reminded of all his good qualities. The power of his voice captured aching hearts and healed wounded emotions after all. And he was perfect in bed.

"Why, J.D. was wild," Delia had said two weeks ago, as she'd offered condolences, "and I know you two always fought like cats and dogs, but it was nice to watch you make up."

Just as J.D. could turn the most humble ingredients into a tasty meal, he could fix any gadget around the house, and draw a bath that was always the right temperature. As Susannah polished off her plate, she recalled the fan letters she'd read after the funeral, especially one by a woman who'd forgiven her two-timing man. Suddenly a dull ache claimed her heart. Her husband's songs had saved marriages on the rocks, mended broken family rifts and soothed lonely people to sleep.

When she finished eating, he said, "Seconds?"

She'd been thinking about how he hadn't really cheated on her. She shook her head and stared down at the empty plate. "I'll do the dishes," she said contritely, and once more, she felt a stabbing little pain of emotion. It had been so long since they'd shared a meal or discussed domestic details like this.

"Don't worry. I'll get them."

She yawned. "What time is it, anyway?"

"Late. About three in the morning."

Fear had kept her alert. "The bewitching hour." Just as she

said the words, she could have kicked herself. She half expected J.D. to say, "Time for some magic, Susannah? Scarves and cards? A touch of my magic wand?"

But he was silent.

Hours ago, she'd been in New York, dressed to the nines and attending an awards ceremony. If she couldn't see the statue on the kitchen counter, she'd scarcely believe it. His eyes followed hers to it, and his jaw clenched. He started to say something, then changed his mind.

After that, it seemed too quiet. The night had settled, just as surely as an old house, and it made her miss Banner Manor. Even insects and owls had simmered down, as if to better hallow the wee hours. Through a window was low, leafy foliage, making her feel hemmed in and surrounded. She knew better, but she shook her head ruefully, and said what was in her mind. "This reminds me of years ago, back when you were playing local gigs."

He seemed to know what she meant and nodded. "Yeah."

By the time the band had walked off stage, loaded their equipment and arrived home, it was usually about this time. Still keyed up, tired but not ready for sleep, she and J.D. would sit at the kitchen table at Banner Manor, either talking or simply staring at the moon. At some point, he'd take her hand, and they'd go to bed and make love, sometimes until the rose fingers of dawn began touching the windows.

Abruptly, she stood. "I'd best turn in. It was an exciting evening, to say the least." She shot a sudden, tense glance outside. "Do you really think we're safe?"

"Sheriff Kemp says so. Definitely safer than at Banner Manor, I figure. I already checked all the locks." He paused. "Nobody knows about my relationship with Mama Ambrosia."

"I didn't know you were close enough to stay in her house."

He shrugged. "I've been letting her read my cards and tell my fortune since I was a kid."

"And what did it say last time she looked into her crystal ball?"

A cloud passed over his eyes, so she didn't believe him when he said, "I have a bright and rosy future."

"Lucky you. 'Cause she said I was in danger."

"I'm sorry, Susannah," he said softly.

Suddenly she wanted to talk about so many things—about how Robby had treated him tonight, and how easily Sheriff Kemp had taken his reappearance in stride. She wanted to discuss Sandy, too, although she didn't quite know what to say, except that she believed J.D. now. He'd definitely never slept with her. And what about Joel Murray? she thought. Was he really the victim?

Rather than voice her thoughts, she silently nodded and began walking toward the hallway, deciding to let J.D. clean up, since he'd offered.

"Susannah."

He'd spoken so quietly that she almost thought it had been her imagination. It seemed a mere phantom, the way it sounded when she listened to his records sometimes. Like it was simultaneously him and yet not him.

Turning, she leaned against the door frame and arched an eyebrow. "Hmm?"

"I didn't sleep with her. That's all. I want you to believe me. Just about that one thing."

She nodded. When she'd found Sandy lying next to him in bed, she'd been shocked and outraged, not thinking clearly. Sometime later, she'd realized that he'd looked surprised. Because he'd gotten caught, she'd thought at the time. Now she knew that his being in the buff meant nothing; he always slept that way. He'd been shocked to see Sandy there. "Obviously," she managed, "Sandy was obsessed with you."

"I didn't know she was in bed with me."

"I know." She paused. "But you brought some pretty strange people into our lives."

"That's an understatement."

"I'm trying to be kind."

"I didn't leave enough space for just the two of us."

And that had been the real issue. "If it helps, you were right about a lot of things, J.D.," she said, wondering if it even mattered to admit it at such a late stage of the game. "I was never really jealous, not the way you said at Banner Manor. I mean, I didn't think you'd run off with some other woman. But I figured it was only a matter of time until this whole new world you'd entered completely swept you away. It got to where, every time you'd leave to go play, I half expected you not to come back home."

Just as she finished speaking, he got to his feet, circled the kitchen island and strode toward her. When he was a foot away, she could feel his breath and the warmth rising from his bare chest. Her hands yearned to reach for him, her fingers longed to touch. Suddenly, her voice broke. "You were always so much bigger than me, J.D."

"Not so," he returned in a husky whisper, made even sexier because of his slow drawl. "I can't believe what you've done without me, Susannah. I knew you could do it, but the restaurant—"

"It's sad, though," she interjected. "Our lives diverging. I used to think of us as one river, flowing together, but it's like we hit a solid rock, J.D. Now I'm going one way, and you're going another." *If we even survive this,* a tiny voice inside her said. "Only danger brought us back together."

"I'll never let anything happen to you, Susannah."

"Sandy Smithers's actions aren't in your control, J.D."

His lips pursed, just slightly, as if in displeasure, then something dark and unreadable crossed his features. She watched the lips part, a fraction, and in the silence, she heard a release of breath that sounded strangely labored. All at once, she was aware of promise, desire and hope. Something quickened inside her, sparking and igniting, flowing through her veins, and beneath her top, she could feel the arousal of her unrestrained breasts. The cotton chaffed against her taut nipples.

Heat surged to her extremities, and she felt a blush rising on her cheeks. Inadvertently, her eyes dropped hungrily over her husband, his hairy chest and the inny belly button of his flat belly.

When he spoke, his voice sounded hoarse, almost strangled, as if he'd reached some sort of breaking point. "You'd better go to bed, Susannah."

Her gaze found his, locking on intense, searing blue eyes. His chest gave away his desire by rising and falling just a little too quickly. She could see the pulse at his throat, the tip of his tongue when it darted out to touch his lips, as if licking away their dryness.

"You'd really better go to bed, Susannah," he repeated.

Although she knew better, she found herself whispering, almost against her will, "Alone, J.D.?"

12

ALONE?

J.D didn't figure she wanted to make love—not tonight, not ever. But her eyes affirmed her feelings, looking hyperalert, narrowing to shining slits the color of lakes under sunlight. He saw hesitation, then frank sexual arousal, which he shared.

"Dammit," he muttered under his breath. "Can't you see how hard this is for me, Susannah?"

"Hard on you?" she echoed.

"You, too," he conceded. Still, had she confronted the fears about his traveling and other woman he'd known she harbored during their marriage? He exhaled heavily, and planted his palm on the door frame beside her head. Without moving, he could feel the still-damp strands of her hair, and he imagined how sensual they'd feel stroking the sensitive spaces between his fingers. He felt breathless, as if some robber, hell-bent on stealing his heart, had just duct-taped his ribs so it couldn't escape.

He could smell her body, too, fresh and musky from a shower, scented with apple-blossom soap. She'd pulled a half-zipped hoodie over a plain white T-shirt. She was braless—obviously so, since the cotton fabric of the shirt stretched taut between her breasts. The relaxed nipples were visible, tempting him, making him sharply aware of the painful, irre-sistible pang bothering his groin. Like the badgering voice of some annoying harpie, the irritation wasn't going to abate, he knew, not unless he got some of the satisfaction only this woman could give.

Which he wasn't. And that meant there was no use driving himself crazy with lust. When he found his voice, it was less steady than before, throatier and carrying a steely undercurrent of raw frustration that he didn't even bother to try to conceal. Why should he when it was evident in the slight forward thrust of his hips, his elevated respiration, the sharpness of his roving gaze. "C'mon—" He didn't enjoy sounding as if he were begging, but maybe he was. "Just go to bed, Susannah."

She didn't move immediately, and he knew she must be as needy as he. Not that she'd give in to temptation. She was merely toying with him right now by offering him sex. Soon enough she'd spurn him, then ask for a divorce again. And he wasn't about to let her do it. "You're not taking me to the edge, then changing your mind," he said softly.

"You think that's what I'm doing?"

"Oh yeah."

When she inhaled sharply, then held her breath as if suppressing a telltale shudder, he felt completely breathless, himself. Instinctually his gaze dropped in time to see her nipples constrict, the nipples beading against the white cotton, forming delicious pert points. He gritted his teeth, trying to brace himself, but it didn't stop the liquid fire that shot between his legs, making him feel heavy and swollen and as if he was losing his mind.

He was like a gun and she was the target, and he was fully loaded and ready to shoot. Every inch of her was begging for his fingers and tongue. As heat continued pouring into his groin, he reflexively clenched his teeth once more against the unwanted sensations.

Her voice was husky. "Do you really want me to go to bed, J.D.?"

"Yes and no." She might as well be teasing him with a strip number, and she knew it. Just looking at those aroused breasts was almost as bad as seeing her in the wet dress earlier.

Truth be told, in the past eight months, he hadn't so much as looked at another woman. And right now, he wanted sex so bad he could taste it. With her. Each nip and tuck had been visible, the fabric clinging like a second skin. Now, she hadn't even touched him, and he had to fight not to shut his eyes and let them roll back in his head in ecstasy just from the memory. He felt—really felt—the delicious tension between his legs, the fiery pulse of the erection increasingly worrying his zipper.

No doubt she was reading his mind, the way she always had. Not that it was all that hard to read. He was a hundred-percent male, so what he was thinking wasn't very complex. "This would hardly be the first time we've felt a little hot but managed to avoid sex," he finally offered, the words gruff.

She didn't say anything.

"Hell, Susannah," he added, really wishing she'd leave him alone, "Sexual avoidance had become the hallmark of our marriage, anyway." He paused raising his eyes to hers. "And there it is again," he accused. "That spark of challenge in your eyes. You'd make love to me just to prove you'll always have that power over me, wouldn't you?"

Her lower lip trembled, either from pique or passion, he wasn't sure which. "Of course not, J.D. I just had a weak moment," she assured him, turning away.

He couldn't control his movements; his hand found her shoulder. For a second, he was sure he'd draw her closer, saw himself grasping her hand and bringing it between his legs, where he wanted to feel it…had to feel it. "Contain it then," he said huskily, his words a soft warning as she turned to face him again. "Don't start this, Susannah."

"Start what?"

As if she didn't know. "You're being intentionally difficult."

The slight smile that touched her lips was too much like a smirk, and he suddenly wanted to kiss it away. "Is that what I am...difficult?"

And so much more. His gaze dropped to her breasts again, then to the curve of her belly, and he suppressed an urge to mold his hands over her hips. Already he could feel his hands tightening against her flesh, the shock of desire when he pressed her pelvis to his. "I thought you wanted a divorce."

"What's that got to do with you and me having sex?"

Nothing maybe. Everything. Despite his determination to start behaving like the gentleman he'd never been before, he muttered, "Start what, you say?" He eyed her. "Be careful how you ask questions like that, Susannah, because I might decide to answer you, and my answer won't be in words."

"You and your idle threats, J.D.," she drawled slowly, shrugging his hand off her shoulder and turning to leave. "Forgive me if I had a lapse in judgment. That should be understandable, given how long we were married. But don't take it personally. I just haven't been with a man for a while."

"Joe?"

"We never...went all the way."

But they'd done other things. Even if he hadn't seen them kissing while he'd spied at her restaurant, he'd have intuited it from her gaze now. The thought of it made him want to leave his mark, remind her of their past. And it he felt doubly frustrated since he'd been as celibate as a monk.

His hand closed over her upper arm now, and he yanked her closer, his heart pounding uncontrollably when her chest brushed his, electrifying his blood, making it dance, even after she leaned away from the contact. Every fiber of his being awakened.

A malicious glint sparked in her eyes, or maybe he just imagined it. "Anyway, I guess Joe is my business."

"Payback?" he guessed. "For Sandy?"

"It didn't have anything to do with her."

His grip tightened, and the tense, whipcord lash of his lean body hardened against hers. Thighs met thighs and he let her feel how hard he was. He tried to take a deep, steadying breath. Somehow things had gotten turned on their head. His supposed affair wasn't the issue, but hers was. He had to ask again. "You didn't sleep with him?"

"Would it matter?"

"How could you even ask?"

The room seemed utterly still. She was pressed against him. His heart was hammering hard. Suddenly, heat exploded inside him, bursting into flames as surely as his boat. One kiss, he thought, and he'd be just as devastated. He'd blow sky high and to smithereens. Nothing would remain except splinters and dust washed up on some sandy shore. Dammit, he'd be a pile of ash. Susannah would sweep him up as if she were Cinderella.

It was funny. The destroyed boat was the perfect symbol for their marriage, wasn't it? Beautiful and sleek, lovingly crafted and nurtured, and now dashed on the rocks. If the music world didn't think he was dead, maybe he'd write a song about it.

"I didn't sleep with him," she said. "He's seeing someone else. Does that make you happy?"

"I tried to tell myself it did," he admitted slowly, drawing out each vowel. "I kept thinking you deserved better than me, better than what I brought into our lives. And now, with Sandy out there somewhere…?" He shook his head. "Dammit," he muttered, interrupting his own train of thought. "I hope she's the one who blew up the *Alabama*, not someone else…"

Susannah sounded surprised. "Why?"

"Because if it's not her, they'll have to start the investigation over from scratch." God only knew the enemies he'd unknowingly fostered. He sighed, wishing the maddening scent of apple blossoms wasn't knifing from Susannah to his lungs again. The scent was cloying, enveloping him as if in a cloud, reminding him he was trapped with a woman who didn't love him anymore.

"I kept telling myself I didn't care," he continued, picking up his earlier thread, "and now I'm starting to remember what our marriage was really like."

"I'd divorce you," she offered in a deceptively light tone, pressing closer, teasing him with her lower body, tilting her chin as if to better peer into his eyes. "But it's hard to get a dead man to sign legal papers."

"I'm sure you'll find a way," he muttered. "Otherwise you've become quite the heiress."

That was a strike to her honor, and the response was quick and hot. "All I ever wanted was Banner Manor!"

And he'd refused to give it, saying possession was ninetenths of the law. He'd done so, since once Banner Manor was gone, Susannah would be gone, too. "Just go to bed," he said again, although his own hand was what stayed her.

When he finally released his hold, only her eyes moved, drifting down his bare chest as if she'd hadn't dared to hope she'd see it again. Unbidden, images from his funeral assaulted him—her tears, the silly hunting hat she'd carried, which he'd taken from the house later, and put into his bag as a reminder of her love. He recalled her softening expression when he'd handed her his handkerchief tonight, too, and the loosening of her body when she'd given in and let him carry her through the rain.

"We'll talk tomorrow," he said, his chest feeling impossibly constricted, almost as tight as his jeans.

"About?"

Everything. He shrugged. "Sandy. The boat. Whether it was Joel onboard. All the real reasons we're together. The truth is, if you weren't in danger, we'd never have seen each other again."

"Not so. You came to the house, J.D., long before you saw the contents of Sandy's bag."

He settled on saying, "I care about your well-being, Susannah. I can't have you hurt because of something I've done. I'm going to protect you. Then you can go your own way. I'll go mine."

"Where are you going? Back to the grave?"

As always, she was as impertinent as hell. And usually right. "I'll...fix that, somehow."

She stared into his eyes, her gaze unnervingly inscrutable. "Why? Because you're a changed man. Right, J.D.?"

He'd told her so, hadn't he? And yet how many times had he vowed he was turning over a new leaf only to prove himself wrong? He wanted to say yes, but it would be a lie. "I don't know. Only time will tell."

"Well it looks like we've got plenty of that on our hands."

"And what are you suggesting?" he bit out, his gaze lacerating hers because of the cheapness of what she seemed to be implying. "That we spend our time here in bed? Have a little roll in the hay? A tumble for old time's sake?" He paused a fraction closer, his lips registering her breath. "Do you want me to get mad? To feel I have to prove what I can do to you? That I get you so hot you're begging me?"

"It's what you want, isn't it?"

"No, it's what you want." His hands moved of their own accord, and they rested on her shoulders. Suddenly, he felt twisted into knots, utterly confused. "Hell yes, I want it," he admitted, his voice low, the scalding heat flooding his loins forcing him to tell the truth. "I never stopped wanting it. Never stopped wanting you. Maybe I never will, Susannah. But that's not the point."

"Which is?"

That unless they were getting back together, he didn't want to risk loving her physically. It would only lead to emotional pain later. He settled for answering with a sigh.

"If you really care about my safety," she said calmly, "then why not just hire a real bodyguard?"

She was right. Hell, what had he been thinking? He'd hired a pilot, after all. Besides, a bodyguard wouldn't have to see him or know he was alive. But in Sheriff Kemp's office, J.D. hadn't considered that, had he? He'd been too intent on what might happen when he was alone with Susannah in the cabin. "Tomorrow, I'll do just that."

"Glad that's settled," she said firmly.

He could scarcely breathe. "Good night, Susannah."

"Good night, J.D."

When she turned stiffly on her heel, he felt heartsick. Worse when his gaze settled on her backside. A backlash of lust claimed him as the gaze traveled slowly down her long legs. What was wrong with him? Any normal man would have taken her offer. He tried to shake himself loose of the physical sensations rocking his body, but he couldn't.

She disappeared down the hallway into her room and he dragged a hand through his hair and headed toward the sink, lifting the dirty plates. As he washed them, he got his mind off of her by staring through the kitchen window. Slivers of silver moonlight were making their way through the thick trees now. Otherwise, it was silent. If anyone was out there, he figured he'd sense it.

But he hadn't realized Sandy might be dangerous before. He pushed aside the admonishment, his hawklike eyes scanning Mama Ambrosia's yard. It was tempting to rifle through her herbs, but he was fairly certain there was nothing there to quell his current problem—lust. As soft as it was, the sudsy dish water could have been her hair. The room's darkness, when he shut off the kitchen light, could have been the midnight of her eyes.

Then he heard her bedroom door shut. Thankfully, his hard-on was subsiding. Somewhat. Maybe enough that he could sleep. He'd be damned if he was going to give in and pleasure himself, not when his wife was right down the hall. Sighing, he rechecked the locks on the doors and windows, then headed down the hallway, deciding to leave on that light, in case Susannah had to find the bathroom in the night.

He didn't bother with the light in his own room; the hallway was casting a soft yellow glow over it. He'd chosen the most modest room, decorated only with a twin iron bed, a chest at the foot and a nightstand beside it. If he'd picked the smallest room to punish himself for what he'd done to Susannah, it wasn't going to help. Moonlight was slanting through the window, and although it was muted by pines and oaks, it was decidedly romantic. Exhaling another long sigh, he moved toward the bed.

Just as he reached it, he heard a click, then footsteps. Susannah. She was coming down the hallway. Not knowing what to expect, he turned around. Still dressed, she'd slipped on some rubber flip-flops that Robby had brought her.

Thinking of his ex-best friend, he felt a stab of pain, but he pushed it away. "Do you need something, Susannah?"

"Yeah." She was framed in the doorway, her face in shadows. "Sex," she said simply. "I can't be in the same house with you and not have sex, J.D." When he didn't respond immediately, she added, "I hate myself for it."

This conversation was getting ridiculous, he decided. "Well, I'd hate for you to hate yourself."

"Nice of you."

"If it's any consolation," he said, his gaze drifting over her. "You can't hate yourself as much as I hate myself."

"And why do you hate yourself?"

"For putting you in this mess."

Something vaguely resembling a smile curved her lips in the semi-darkness, lifting his spirits, reminding him of how things used to be between them. The moonlight helped, touching her face like fingers, illuminating the partial smile.

"Since we're in mutual hate, we might as well do it," she said reasonably.

That was just like Susannah. Sex first, talk later. It was the kind of behavior of which she always accused him. They were more alike than she knew, he decided, not that he'd tell her. He considered a long moment. "Misery loves company," he finally said.

"That's exactly what I was thinking."

"Well, since strong emotion is always key in the bedroom, whether it's love or hate may be immaterial at the moment," he conceded. He'd let her take the lead. Hell, this was her big idea, right? And every move he made seemed to turn out wrong. "Should we move to the big bed? Your call."

He could see her throat working as she swallowed hard. It

must have been hard for her to come back and proposition him again, he suddenly realized.

"The little bed's fine," she said.

She must be damn aroused, he thought, if she couldn't allow time to move to a more comfortable locale. Or else she wanted to make sure the bed was his, since that way, she could leave when she liked. "Less time to change your mind?"

"Closer proximity."

"I'm taking no responsibility for this," he warned, crossing his arms over his bare chest. "So the first move is yours."

"And after that?"

"After that—" He shook his head. "I can't vouch for a thing."

His heart stuttered as she crossed the room, and he took in all the nuances—the careful steps, the swing of unconfined breasts, the trembling fingers.

She stopped in front of him. "What are you looking at me like that for?"

His hands settled on her shoulders once more, and he simply pulled her close, his lips brushing her hair. Drowning in the scent, he nuzzled, his voice lowering to a hoarse whisper. "I'm gauging how you want it."

"Want what?"

"You know."

"And how do I want it?"

"Maybe slow or fast," he murmured, pressing his mouth deeper against nearly dry strands of silken hair that teased his lips like the most intense kiss. "Or hard and deep…or gentle and playful."

"It's been awhile. You'll have to remind me."

His hands slipped from her shoulders, pushing off the hoodie, and as she started shrugging out of it, he became aware of his groin once more. It ached, his erection straining with this promise of coming satisfaction. Still, she'd taken him near the brink before and walked away, leaving him hot, angry and frustrated. But this time…

Sucking air through clenched teeth, he dragged the hoodie down her long, bare arms, leaving only the T-shirt. "Teasing," he murmured, inching back a fraction to glance down the length of her body. Lust surged when he realized she probably wasn't wearing any underwear. Soon he'd find out.

Lifting both hands, he pinched the nipples through her shirt, watching in fascination as the already constricted buds performed, growing more taut as he toyed, rolling them between his thumb and finger. As he watched her face—how it filled with rapture—he jutted out his lower lip, then bit down on it hard, his buttocks tightening, his hips tilting.

Lightly he brushed his jeans against her pants, reveling in the puzzle-piece fit of his hardness to where she was so soft, and he bit down on his lip even harder, almost hard enough to draw blood. Again and again, he pulled her nipples, plucking them like flowers. Still pinching, he moved them in slow circles, soliciting a soft whine that stirred his blood.

"Hard and hot," she whispered.

"Not gentle like this?" He was still teasing, sweeping his lower body against hers, letting her feel the heat trapped inside his jeans. Suddenly it was too much. His hands rustled the shirt upward and abruptly covered her bare breasts, kneading as he roughly whispered, "So you want to play some scarves and cards, Susannah?"

"I want to get so hot that I vanish," she whispered back as his mouth claimed hers.

A sunburst exploded, undoing whatever thread was holding him together. He plunged and plundered with his tongue, stroked her cheeks and tasted her teeth. As his hands explored the sides of her breasts, the slopes and cleavage, he knew wanted to remain dead to the world forever. He never wanted to return. Susannah and a cabin was all he wanted. By the time he found her nipples again, his wet tongue kiss had driven her to distraction. She was bucking.

And then her tongue lashed wildly to his like a sail in a storm. It flickered quickly like a guttering flame in wind. He thought of the many times he'd felt that tongue elsewhere…on his neck, his belly, between his legs. Now it pushed deeper between his lips, the passion a wave held back by a breaking dam.

"Abracadabra," he whispered huskily, his mouth trailing her jaw, the column of her throat. Then hungrily, he added, "Take your pants off."

"Why don't you take them off me, J.D.?"

"Gladly." Turning, he grabbed her hand, twining it through his as he half dragged her to the bed. "You said you want the little bed," he growled, his jeans bursting at the seams. "Fine by me. But you'd better get on it."

She didn't argue, only scrambled onto the mattress, settling by the headboard. His mind went blank, and he could only stare. She had an angel's face, and her chest was heaving against the see-through T-shirt, which was still pushed above her breasts.

With a grunt, he undid his belt buckle, then with a gasp, he opened the snap and pulled down the zipper, wincing when it raked skin. Pushing the pants over his hips, he stepped out of them just as she grabbed the hem of her shirt. She pulled it over her head, her ravenously hungry blue eyes shining with desire as they fixed on his aroused body, making him doubly aware of his burning erection.

Nearly dry now, her tawny strands of hair, which he'd mussed, cascaded over her bare, glowing shoulders, looking as golden as the pants she wore in the low light. Blindly he moved toward the bed. When he reached her, he threaded a hand into the gorgeous blond strands, dragging her upward to take his mouth. She tilted her head to give him access, her back arching with uncanny suppleness, bending over his arm, and this time, when his lips closed over hers, she seemed to know the kiss wouldn't end.

With his tongue, he built the fire raging inside, his practiced hands grabbing the drawstring of her pants, then urging the fabric over her long legs as smooth as glass. Just as masterfully, her hands nestled between his legs, and when her fingers circled him, his mind blanked once more. Blackness overtook him, leaving him with just a cloud of sensation.

But he kept driving his tongue between her lips, thrusting, although his thoughts were breaking apart. He didn't give a damn that they were divorcing. Didn't care if he never saw her again. All he cared about was right now. This second. His whole energy was focused on the moment.

It was sheer bliss. She was stroking him slowly. Fingers curled in his pubic hair, then fondled the shaft. Fisting, she squeezed until perspiration coated his skin. His wife had lost her girlish fears of appearing too brazen years ago, and she could pleasure a man as boldly as he'd pleasure himself. Now, confidently, she was pushing him to the edge, and his head snapped, veering backward.

His lips found her mouth, slamming down greedily. He was gasping between kisses. Suddenly, his hand stayed hers. But he was powerless, and his palm merely slid over the back of her hand, guiding her movements.

"Stop," he whispered.

She did, knowing he could take no more. A second later, he was on top of her. There were no condoms, but it wouldn't matter. They'd had no other lovers, and they'd never been able to get pregnant, not even after seeing a doctor. That had bothered him more than Susannah ever knew. Surely, if she loved him more, she'd have their baby, he'd thought when they were trying, however illogically.

Now he counted his blessings. She hated him. She craved his body but she hated him. And he didn't blame her. No, he didn't…

But he craved her. He ran a splayed hand from her breasts to her ribs. Releasing a shuddering sigh, he pressed his mouth to her belly. Every inch was so damn silken. Like air or water. As soft as soap. His fingers twined into her damp, springy lower curls. His middle finger, curled and dipped, and what he felt next undid his last shred of resistance.

She was wet…so impossibly wet. The kind of wet that meant she was on the edge. One touch and she might come. And so, abruptly, he thrust harder, breaking the kiss so he could watch her neck tilt in pleasure, her eyes roll back. She arched and squirmed, and he leaned closer, panting on the wet kisses he'd trailed on her skin.

His gaze roved over her. Her lips, drenched from kisses a second before, turned dry, and she licked them senselessly. And licked. And licked…

"Maybe I won't let you come," he teased.

"Damn you, J.D.," she whispered, her breath uneven, her eyes glazed and dreamy, the expression naked.

Curving his finger, he lifted moisture and drizzled it around her clitoris. She was still uttering soft little cries as he moved on top of her again. Looking down into her face, she drove both hands into his chest hair. Grabbing fistfuls of dark curls that glistened with perspiration, she raked nails down his bare flesh.

"You know what that does to me," he whispered.

"Not as much as this," she whispered back, her legs parting.

"Or this," he agreed, penetrating her with ease. Her hands flew upward, and he shuddered as her fingers clutched his shoulders. She was tensing, bracing herself. But he rested. Waited. Let her feel every inch.

Glorious relief claimed him at being enveloped in his wife's encapsulating heat. Maybe she wouldn't be that tomorrow. Or next year. Or whenever she got her way and divorced him. But tonight she was still his wife. Legally. And he would remind her of it.

On her chest, he laid the heel of a palm, settling it between her breasts. Having realized the Saint Christopher's medal wasn't his, she'd removed it, and that touched his heart. She might not love him the way she once had, but she'd meant to wear a reminder of him forever. Now he examined the other necklace she wore. Engraved on it were the words, *Remember the time*.

"That's what I want you to do right now, Susannah," he murmured.

She sounded far away as if the connection of their bodies was taking her to some faraway place. "What?"

"Remember the times," he whispered.

She stared into his eyes in the moonlight. "Which times?"

There were so many. "All of them."

"Help me remember," she whispered.

And so he thrust hard, pushing deeper, opening her completely, making her gasp, pushing her upward on the mattress until her head collided with pillows.

Sheathed inside, buried deep, he lay skin to skin, motionless. And then slowly, torturously, he rolled his hips, grinding, prompting endless whimpers until she convulsed. As he felt fluttering palpitations, his eyes remained fixed on her face, the softening of her jaw, the parting of her lips for another kiss.

He could have let go then. Everything had vanished. Outside, the night was nearly gone. It, too, had peaked, and was sliding towards dawn. Shots of gray were mixing with yellow moonlight. He should have been tired, but he wasn't, only hopelessly aroused. Sandy and Joel were far away, as was the mystery surrounding the *Alabama*. Hell, he was no cop, he thought vaguely. Let the law figure out what had happened. J. D. Johnson had other troubles at the moment…woman troubles.

When Susannah's eyelids batted open, his stomach did a somersault, tumbling into oblivion. And when her gaze found his, she looked as if she couldn't decide what to say. He was still throbbing inside her, hard and burning. He was about to explode, his body blistering and slick with sweat.

"You always did have more control than me, J.D.," she finally whispered.

He couldn't help but smile, just a wry grin that upturned the edges of his lips. Even more amazing, she smiled back. It was dazzling, he decided. From day one, it had stopped him in his tracks, hadn't it? Her white teeth gleamed in the near dark, and the smile turned a little saucy.

Somehow, he found his voice, such as it was. "It's not a contest, Susannah."

"No?"

"Maybe," he conceded, still smiling. He leaned to whisper the next words into her ear, his slow drawl drizzling. "But since I just won the first round, maybe you'll stand a better chance in the future, wife of mine."

"We're getting divorced," she reminded him throatily, but at the moment, her heart wasn't in the fight.

"Not tonight, though. And since we're still married, you have some conjugal duties to fulfill."

Lifting a finger, she pressed it to his lips and murmured, "Then let's not waste time talking, J.D."

"You always were a wise woman," he agreed. It was why he'd married her. Leaning a fraction closer, he nipped her earlobe. Releasing a sudden shudder, he thrust again. "Hard and fast this time," he whispered simply. "Tonight you're mine."

Tomorrow was another day.

13

"OH, SUSANNAH, now don't you cry for me," J.D. sang. Bare-chested, since she was using his plaid shirt for warmth, he was wearing yesterday's jeans and a tawny Stetson hat. He was propped on one elbow in the grass and settled his free hand on her belly.

"I'm not crying, J.D.," she drawled, as he glided a hand beneath the hem of her T-shirt, stroking her ribs as if they were strings of his guitar. At times, since last night, she'd thought she might cry, of course. Now, hearing him sing rekindled her passion. They'd slept most of the day, and when she'd opened her eyes to the afternoon sun and realized his kisses were tickling her awake, she'd felt at peace.

It couldn't last, it never did, but sometime after sunup, they'd switched to the bigger bed, and she'd sprawled in it luxuriously, yawning and stretching. The eight and a half months since she'd left J.D. seemed like a silly dream, as did all the characters who'd peopled their lives temporarily, such as Sandy and Maureen and Joel.

But they weren't mere figments, Susannah reminded herself, fear edging into her consciousness. Joel was probably dead, and even if Sandy wasn't responsible for the explosion aboard the *Alabama*, she'd maliciously destroyed pictures of Susannah, written about how much she hated her and possibly fired the shots in New York. How could such a gorgeous woman have gotten so scrambled? Men were still dredging the river, looking for evidence near the explosion she might have caused.

"Given the magnitude of the blast, it'll take time," Sheriff Kemp had said the previous night. "Now that we know the boat's destruction wasn't accidental, Bayou Blair's offering more manpower."

Not that Susannah blamed Sheriff Kemp. He was a small-town sheriff, unused to crimes of this caliber and danger-ously understaffed. "It's not your fault," Susannah had assured him. "Before this, J.D.'s antics were the worst thing you've had to deal with."

Shaking off the memories, Susannah surveyed J.D., smiling at his bad-boy grin. As usual, the man was congratu-lating himself on how well he'd satisfied her in bed. Not that he didn't deserve to preen. About an hour earlier, they'd finished making love again, this time in the grass under a romantic, lacy canopy of leaves, before they'd dressed again.

"What if somebody's watching," she'd protested as they'd first taken off their clothes.

He'd looked enticing in the buff, sunlight shimmering on a pelt of sleek black chest hair, his skin glowing. "We're safe," he'd assured.

Probably that had been his hormones talking. She glanced around. "I don't feel watched, the way I have sometimes over the past few weeks," she admitted. "But Sandy could show up, don't you think? I mean, if she's responsible for every-thing that's happened, she's capable of anything. And she *was* in our house."

"Yes, she was," J.D. agreed soberly.

"She could have seen…" Susannah's voice trailed off.

"Something to connect you to Mama Ambrosia. Or overheard you making an appointment to get your cards read."

"Impossible," he assured her. "I would just show up."

She smirked, feeling relieved. "Very like you."

"I'll make appointments in the future," he promised contritely. "Months in advance. First thing in the morning, too, preferably before 7:00 a.m."

"Unlikely."

"Anyway," he added. "Mama Ambrosia's on vacation."

"I wonder where she went." From what little Susannah knew about Mama, it was hard to guess.

"Vegas," he supplied. "She said she was going to drive herself to the airport in Bayou Blair, then fly to a fortune teller's convention. At least that's what she told me. I kid you not."

"A fortune-teller's convention?" Susannah chuckled, the cloud passing. She thought of the bedding strewn in the hallway. "We'd better clean her cabin before she gets back."

"She's not due for a week. And I'm not making the bed yet. What's the point when you're going to mess it up again?"

"Me?"

"I'll help," he promised. "Just to be nice."

"Same old J.D.," she complained, now considering his housekeeping habits. Yet she believed he'd changed. He hadn't touched one drop of whisky, although Mama had plenty.

"Oh, Susannah," he sang again. "Don't you cry for me."

She offered a lopsided grin. "Oh, boo-hoo."

"You might not be crying now," he warned, his gaze searing and lazy as he tapped her nose with the blade of grass, then leaned to kiss her. "But you were last night. And a minute ago."

"After a fashion," she conceded as he delivered a slow, languid kiss, then stood, grabbed her hand and hauled her to her feet, pausing so she could slip into her flip-flops. Just as she shoved her feet into them, she gasped. "You!"

He chuckled.

He'd changed the position of her shoes, the way he always did, and they'd wound up on the wrong feet. "You're juvenile. You know that, J. D. Johnson?" she accused, lifting his shirt from the ground and handing it to him. "Put that on," she added when he merely slung the shirt over his shoulder.

"C'mon," he said. "I haven't got all the sex out of my system yet. But next time, I want to do it in a bed again. Then for supper, I'll make you some pan-fried spiced chili that will really make you weep."

"Hmm. I see you have my whole life planned out."

"Only the good parts."

"You're definitely the same old Jeremiah Dashiell. And it's just like you to lace everything with cayenne."

"I'm a hot guy," he returned, playfully swatting her behind as they walked through the woods, toward the cabin, their bodies moving together perfectly.

"Hmm. Or you have to doctor the taste of your cooking."

"I'm the best cook in Mississippi and you know it." He shot her a saucy grin. "As for doctoring, my lovin' is the best medicine, sweetheart."

"Then why are you not cured yet?" She squinted at him. "Are you sure you didn't use one of Mama's herbs on me last night?"

"I put some love potion in that steak," he admitted. "But don't you call me that."

"What?" she asked innocently as the cabin appeared, winking through the trees. "Jeremiah Dashiell?"

Resettling the Stetson on his head, he shot her a lopsided grin. "Just don't tell anybody."

"And if I do?"

He winked. "I've got special ways of punishing you."

Truth be told, she secretly liked the name, so the words were out before she'd thought them through. "If we'd had a baby, J.D., that's what I would have named it."

Too late, she saw his eyes widen. She could swear she saw a flicker of hope there, but he didn't miss a beat. "Well then, it's a good thing that baby we didn't have wasn't a girl."

She couldn't help but chuckle. "A girl named Jeremiah Dashiell?"

"Well, Johnny Cash did okay with a boy named Sue," he offered with a smile, referring to the title of a famous Johnny Cash song.

Her chest tightened, her heart breaking at the reminder of her husband's music career. He'd always had music on the brain, and she'd wanted children just as desperately. Who knew where things were heading now? In the past twenty-four hours neither of them had said much about their marriage.

This is just about sex, she tried to remind herself. They were never going to share their lives again. In fact, she'd been a fool to succumb to his charms last night and this morning. And yet, she'd come onto him, hadn't she? Could she really let him go?

J.D. tilted his head. "Is that my phone?"

She didn't hear anything.

He patted the pocket of the shirt draped over his shoulder. "I was sure I brought it." Flashing another heart-stopping smile as he speeded his steps, he said, "You distracted me."

"Guilty as charged," she returned.

As they raced for the phone, she thought he looked gorgeous, as carefree as in the past, the wind riffling his thick, dark hair, the sun glistening in the strands, his toned muscles rippling. They entered the cabin, and just as he reached the cell, which was on the bedside table in the smaller bedroom, the ringing stopped. Immediately, another shrill ring sounded from the front room.

"Mama's phone?"

It rang only once. As they reached the answering machine in the front room, it clicked on. Sheriff Kemp's voice was urgent. "I just tried the cell. Pick up if you're there."

Susannah sprang forward, but J.D. reached the phone first and snatched the receiver. "We're here."

Sheriff Kemp was talking loudly, but Susannah leaned closer to hear him anyway, almost just to be nearer to J.D. "You should probably get out of there," the sheriff said. "I'm on my way with Robby and some men from Bayou Blair. I'm calling from my car."

J.D.'s eyebrows raised in alarm. "What's wrong?"

"Early this morning, we used Robby's key to get into Banner Manor. You're right. The pistol that's supposed to be in your closet is gone." Sheriff Kemp continued, "But it gets worse."

"Worse?"

"Your truck's still at the garage, so we went over it, and the fuel line was cut, just as you suspected. Turns out this woman's military trained, J.D. We just found out. She did a tour during the Gulf War, so she knows how to shoot and plenty about explosives.

"Her folks were glad to hear somebody found her. They've been searching for months. Said they felt let down by the army's response to their troubles. They tapped their own resources to hire a private detective to find their daughter."

"Unbelievable," J.D. whispered, then wolf whistled.

Susannah merely shook her head, shocked.

"Her folks told me Sandy just wasn't right after she got back in country," the sheriff continued. "Whatever she saw overseas scrambled her head, and she wound up hospitalized. Doctors said it was post-traumatic stress, but her folks said she'd been better lately. Then suddenly she took off, leaving a note saying she had found a new mission. She was in love and hitchhiking South to see her new boyfriend." The sheriff paused, then added, "I guess she meant you, J.D."

"Oh, no," Susannah whispered as her mind registered the tragedy. All at once, she remembered a different Sandy. Not the extremely pretty, model-thin groupie, but the wan woman with haunted eyes. Sandy had seemed tough, too, well-muscled for being so thin, but Susannah had assumed she'd worked out, not gone to boot camp. Maybe that also explained the fatigue print clothes she wore with combat boots. For many in the music scene, such styles were seen to be trendy, but for Sandy, it was apparently more....

"Whoa," J.D. was saying. "Sandy must have made a point to meet somebody close to me, in the studio or the band..."

"Joel," Susannah supplied.

"Well, everybody says she's a beauty," Sheriff Kemp put in. "A real knockout."

Still could a complete stranger walk into the home of a famous man without anyone protesting? It was a testament to how uncontrolled their lives had become. Susannah considered what she knew about her own husband's hormones, and she supposed it was possible. Sandy was truly beautiful, and J.D. had said Joel was lonely, without family. If a girl as hot as Sandy had shown interest, Joel might not have asked questions. Because he had played music for so long, people naturally accepted his girlfriend.

Susannah sighed. She and Ellie had been confused about whether Joel and Sandy had even been a couple because the relationship had seemed one-sided. Now it made sense. Sandy had seemed distant, but Joel followed her around like a puppy dog. All the while, Sandy had only wanted to get close to J.D.

Gasping, Susannah instinctively reached for J.D. as if to steady herself. His arm slipped around her waist, feeling comfortable and familiar, making her pulse accelerate. "Maybe Joel found Sandy in bed with you, too," she whispered. She thought of her niece, Laurie. "That could be why he came close to having sex with Laurie—he wanted revenge." *Just like J.D. accused me of doing with Joe.* And wasn't there some truth in it? Wasn't that why she'd run to New York? To get back at J.D. for making such a mess of their lives? Foolishly her own mind had been so fixated on J.D. that she'd hardly noticed all the tiny details.

Now they were adding up.

The sheriff was saying, "Sandy was trained in field work, and knew how to ingratiate herself. Her ex-commander said she was being groomed to spy. She's apparently very smart. He'd hoped she'd wind up working overseas in an embassy capacity."

He paused, adding as if in afterthought, "Ellie's still at Joe O'Grady's. She's fine. She told Robby she didn't want to see him and for him to stay put. So he's in the car behind me. We're almost to Mama Ambrosia's. Some guys are going to fan out over the property and check it out.

"Oh. And the body onboard *was* Joel's," he finished. "I was going to tell you when we got there. But we found..." the sheriff's voice trailed off "...more remains. Dental fragments. Since J.D. identified the Saint Christopher's medal, and we have Joel's name now, we were able to make a match."

J.D. squinted. "The case seems to be clearer now, so why are you headed out here?"

Sheriff Kemp's voice was grave. "Because Sandy Smithers landed in Bayou Blair about an hour ago. It might be best for you two to drive into town, stay in my office. There are a couple men there from Bayou Blair. Delia called me from the diner to say hello. She didn't know about the case, but she said a stranger, some woman, just had coffee there. Delia said she was asking about the whereabouts of Mama Ambrosia's."

"Oh, no," Susannah whispered.

"The woman matched Sandy's description," Sheriff Kemp said.

Susannah leaned closer to the phone. "When did she leave Delia's?"

"About ten minutes ago," said the sheriff. "Delia didn't know what was going on, so she gave her directions. Still, you know how hard it is to find Mama's. Even locals get lost."

Small comfort. Sandy had arrived at about the time Susannah and J.D. had been making love. What had they been thinking? Chalk it up to how hot they could still get for each other.

"Didn't anybody check for *credentials*?" Susannah exploded after J.D. hung up. "Didn't somebody know this woman? Didn't you ask, J.D.?"

He was thrusting their few things into his duffel, his expression wan, as if to say he knew his antics had gone too far. He slipped on the Western-style shirt he'd been carrying, resituated the Stetson on his head, then looked at her, the brim of the hat casting a shadow over his eyes. Raw terror then anger, then steely determination flashed in his gaze. As he slung his bag over his shoulder, he turned to face her, looking positively sick. He shook his head. "I thought Maureen checked everybody out. It was her job."

"But you didn't know!" she burst out. And Banner Manor had become a party haven. A free-for-all. A place where dangerous people could walk in the door. "You're famous, J.D.! You have to protect yourself!" she exclaimed, even as the tragedy of Sandy's situation was sinking in. The woman had fought for the country, only to be harmed herself, maybe for life.

Understanding pierced Susannah's awareness. Maybe that's why Sandy had been so attracted to J.D.! His public career had drawn him into a similar arena where everyone around him had their own agenda. By saving him from users, as she believed Susannah to be, she would be saving herself.

"I thought Maureen—"

"You're so trusting!" Susannah interjected, not letting him finish. "Deep down, you're a decent guy, so you think everyone else is the same. But Maureen only cared about one thing," she said with disgust. "And that's the record company's bottom line. She didn't care about you, J.D. None of them did." Except for Sandy, in her own warped way.

"Oh, Susannah," J.D. muttered, stepping closer. "I'd do anything to change this."

For him, seeing the contents of Sandy's bag had been a wake-up call. For once, J.D. didn't want to be involved in the world he'd created any more than she did. "I know," she managed, but she was shaking with anger.

After all, hindsight didn't change a thing. Life threw curve balls that shifted the game. For J.D., the curves had been relatively easy—fame and fortune. Poor Sandy had been dealt the card of a war she hadn't started, and it had scrambled her mind as surely as Mama Ambrosia shuffled a deck to tell her client's fortunes. Now a man who'd cared for her was dead. No…Sandy's fate sure hadn't been the best. But then, neither had been Joel's.

Despite the tragedy, operating as a civilian, Sandy had induced fear, destroyed property and most assuredly a human life. Forgiveness was a strange task, Susannah thought. Given

her circumstances, had Sandy had clear choices? Had J.D.?
Where did responsibility begin and end?

Susannah was no longer sure. As if sensing some deep
hesitation inside her, J.D. drew her close. He felt hard and
hot, every muscle vibrating. Wrapping his arms tightly
around her, he offered a bear hug, and she melted, tilting up
her head just as he angled his down. His lips brushed hers in
a searing promise.

For a brief moment, she shut her eyes, wishing they were
back in the forest again, where they'd been moments before.
With a rush of desperation, she wanted to feel the prickly hairs
of his rock-hard thighs as she straddled him, the rush of heat as
she took him inside her, the greed of his mouth as he devoured
her with a kiss. Even now, she could feel him responding, his
lower body bending to hers, warming and hardening.

"I love you, Susannah," he whispered against her lips.
"More than my own life. You know that. Now, c'mon. I
grabbed our essentials. Let's get to town. We'll be better protected at the sheriff's office."

Nodding, she turned, jogged down the hallway, then
glanced over her shoulder. "Do we have the keys?"

"Kitchen," he returned simply. "I'll get them, but we'd
better leave the door unlocked for the sheriff."

She headed for the front room, the afternoon looking placid
through the windows. Silence bathed the yard, and warm
sunlight splashed through leaves, creating circular patches of
yellow where sunbeams hit the clearings.

She was halfway across the porch when the bang came.

Ducking, she whirled and ran, barreling headfirst into
J.D.'s midsection. He doubled over, turning sideways. "Get
down!" he commanded.

"I tried to save you," a woman screamed as Susannah

dropped and scrambled on her hands and knees across Mama's front room, crouching behind a sofa.

"I tried to help you, but you killed Joel instead. You put him on the boat. You knew! Just before my bomb went off, I saw him! I saw what you did to Joel, J.D.!"

Sandy. Ice flooded Susannah's veins, and her heart hammered. The woman's head was scrambled, all right.

"That's a lie, Sandy," J.D. shouted, making another wave of terror rip through Susannah as he walked farther out on the porch, the tails of his unbuttoned shirt lifting with a sudden slight breeze. "You've got it all wrong."

There was nothing to shield him from a scorned woman wielding a gun. Desperately Susannah wanted to yell at him, to tell him to get down, but the less Sandy was reminded of her presence, the better.

"I didn't want Joel to get hurt," J.D. called out soothingly, in the same tone that had made so many women swoon. "I swear I'm telling the truth."

The woman's voice wavered, filling Susannah with relief. "You are?"

Susannah peeked over the back of the sofa. Far off, through a window, she saw a shadowy figure emerging from between the trees. It was Sandy, aiming a gun—probably his very own pistol—at J.D. "I know you love me, J.D.," she said, her voice strained with pain.

"You're right, I do," J.D. agreed, making Susannah's heart ache. The woman was coming forward now and lowering the gun. She seemed to be lulled by the soft sincerity in J.D.'s voice. That, and how good he looked in worn jeans, a half-open shirt and a cowboy hat.

No doubt though, his songs were what started Sandy's obsession with him. They could work like a force of nature. Now

J.D. raised his voice calling, "But I don't love you the way you most want, Sandy, the way you most need."

The gun came back up.

"You've got to listen to me, Sandy," he coaxed, remaining calm, his hand steady when he tipped the brim of his hat. "You've got to trust me."

She came almost to the porch, lowering the gun once more.

"We'll have a long talk," he promised, his voice seemingly floating, softly rolling like dust in the air. "Just you and me. 'Cause you're right about a lot of things. There are users out there, and if it wasn't for you, I might not have understood that as well as I do now."

Definitely there was truth in that.

"Now, c'mon, honey," he continued. "Why don't you put down the gun? Enough people have gotten hurt. We don't want to hurt anybody else, do we?"

Slowly the woman shook her head. She was close enough that Susannah could see her better. In faded jeans and without makeup, she looked younger and more vulnerable than Susannah remembered. With relief, she watched her bend, as if to place the revolver on the ground.

Suddenly a siren whooped. Then it fell silent.

"Oh, no," Susannah whispered. Unlike J.D.'s silken voice, the sound of the police car served no real purpose, save to alert Sandy. Susannah watched in horror as the other woman's head jerked toward the cars rolling through the trees. There were three—the sheriff's and Robby's, followed by another from Bayou Blair.

Sandy had mobilized and clutched the weapon now. "You lied to me! You called them!" she shrieked, charging J.D., shooting wildly. Windows shattered. Near Susannah, glass jars of herbs cracked. Liquids splashed to the floor.

J.D. dove through the doorway as Sandy's footsteps pounded after him. Susannah would never be able to piece together what happened next—it happened too fast. J.D. leaped, and she heard the others get out of their cars. Susannah saw a flash of fire as Sandy burst into the cabin, but J.D. leaped over the sofa and flung his body over Susannah's, dislodging his hat, which rolled away.

His voice was thunderous. "Don't hurt my wife."

Maybe Sandy understood the truth then, because she stopped and stared at J.D., who was using his body to shield Susannah. Suddenly she dropped the gun. "You'll never quit loving her," she whispered, sounding lost as men burst through the door. Vaguely, in the periphery of her vision, Susannah registered that Robby and Sheriff Kemp were among them.

"Are you all right, Susannah?" Robby shouted.

Men surrounded Sandy and began subduing her, reading her Miranda rights.

"I'm fine," Susannah managed.

J.D. was hauling her to her feet. "Are you sure?"

She nodded, feeling the strength in his hands as they roved over her, checking each inch. "I'm really fine," she repeated, but she knew she was in shock. She cast a glance toward Sandy who looked just as dazed, as if she wasn't quite sure how she'd gotten to the cabin.

Still, Susannah understood the situation perfectly. She'd almost died. J.D. could have been killed, too. The last few minutes had been surreal. And the last straw. She'd been a fool to think she could make their marriage work.

J.D. was swallowing hard. "I can't believe this."

"Me, neither," she said, shaking all over, her heart pounding violently as the police led Sandy outside. Susannah stared at J.D. She knew him inside and out. She loved him, too. There was no denying it. And maybe he'd even changed.

But she had to stay the course.

Her parents would be heartbroken to see her involved in something such as the scene surrounding her. "Eight months ago," she started, her voice dropping to a near whisper, "when I left…" She paused, her heart lodging in her throat, aching. "I wasn't sure, J.D. But now…"

"Oh, God," he whispered, sensing what was coming. "No, Susannah."

"Yes," she returned simply. "Passion only goes so far, J.D. I love you, but I can't live with you."

He shut his eyes. She watched his chest rise and fall as he breathed deeply, trying to steady himself. When he opened his eyes, they looked startlingly blue, impossibly clear, as if he'd just seen the light. He nodded. "I understand."

She could swear she saw moisture in his eyes, and it almost made her change her mind. In all the years that she'd known him, she'd never seen J.D. cry. "I'm sorry," she said hoarsely.

"Me, too," he returned, sounding shaken.

The end was that simple. Not how she'd imagined it at all. No fireworks now. No fanfare. Somehow she turned away. When she and Ellie had decided to leave Bayou Banner, she'd been at this exact same crossroad. But she hadn't been ready. Now she was. She'd started her own life. She had the restaurant.

Don't turn back, she thought as she walked across the threshold of the cabin's front door. If nearly being killed wasn't the last straw, what would be? How much worse could things get? As sorry as she felt for Sandy's troubles, Susannah had to learn how to be less forgiving. She had to think about herself. Surely, June and Ellie would help her. Yes, they'd tell her she was doing the right thing….

She headed off the porch, into the warm sunlight. To her left, another car door slammed, and Susannah's lips parted in surprise as Mama Ambrosia emerged from an SUV. Clad in a long patchwork dress, with a strange turbanlike hat on her head, she grunted as she lumbered toward Susannah.

"Lord," she muttered angrily. "A premonition brought me home. I should have known better than to even pack! Mind you, missy, it's not every day that I get to commune with my fellow fortune-tellers, either. And you ruined it. Everybody at the conference saw this coming—in their crystal balls, cards, dice, you name it. Every single attendee said, 'Mama, you'd better get home.'"

She glared at Susannah. "Why couldn't you two kiss and make up, the way I said," she demanded, "instead of destroying my cute little house? Do you know how hard it is to build contacts so I can get some of those herbs? That's why I had to go to my conference!"

Susannah was fighting the urge to turn around and look for J.D., but he wouldn't follow her, not this time. Her throat ached. "Sorry," she murmured numbly. Then she couldn't help but ask, "What about the gold key? You said there was one in my future."

"Oh, you'll see it eventually. And if you keep asking me about it, I might point out that I didn't charge you for your last reading."

"But…what do you see in the future now?"

"Don't worry," Mama huffed. "You'll do all right without him. That restaurant of yours will wind up as a franchise. But believe me, if I could interfere with that fortunate fate, I would, due to all the trouble you've caused me, ruining my vacation and such."

"Sorry," Susannah said again.

"Oh, please! I forgive you," huffed Mama. "Just not happily. Now git!"

Not knowing what else to say, Susannah walked toward Robby's car to wait for a ride back to town. As she got inside, she better understood how J.D. felt. Without love, victories were hollow. Right now, J.D.'s bronze trophy was just sitting on a counter, next to canisters of herbs. Without love, prizes meant little in the end. Even if Oh Susannah's did become a franchise, she wasn't sure she'd care. Not the way she would have in the past.

She scarcely felt the burning heat of the vinyl on her legs when she sat. Now J.D. would sign the divorce papers without a fight, and if he bothered to announce he was still alive, the world would take him back, at least the part of him that belonged to the world. The part that belonged to Susannah...well, who knew what would happen to that.

Her gaze shifted to Mama's cabin. Everyone was inside, except for a couple men and Sandy. They were circling the side yard, presumably heading to another car. They were only a blur, though, and otherwise, Susannah could see nothing at all as her eyes filled with tears.

14

"SUSANNAH! Get in here!"

Susannah swiped her hands down the thighs of her jeans, and used the back of a wrist to push aside locks of hair that had come loose from her topknot. She kept bustling around the kitchen. "What, Ellie?"

"Hurry up!"

As if she didn't have anything better to do than watch TV at the bar with Ellie, Joe and Tara. "Some of us have to work for a living," she called, unable to believe anything might be more important than clearing the remaining lunch dishes so the wait staff could set up for dinner.

She was desperate to keep busy. No matter what she did, though, she still had J.D. on the brain. She'd done the right thing by leaving him, of course, and she wasn't about to change her mind. But all week, there had been stories in the newspapers claiming he was alive. Apparently the pilot he'd hired to take him to New York, the same one who'd flown them both back to Bayou Banner, had sold the story to a national tabloid. And when the cabbie who'd taken J.D. to her apartment had seen the story, he'd come forward, as well.

"I knew it was him the second I saw him," the man had vowed.

J.D. hadn't surfaced, though. No, J.D. wouldn't, Susannah

fumed now. For days, the press had been interviewing his fans, wanting their thoughts on J.D.'s "resurrection." Many had shown up at Banner Manor, holding vigil, at least according to Delia who'd called to gossip and thank Susannah for all the business she was getting. "This place has nothing on the foot traffic Jim Morrison gets on his grave," she'd vowed. And since her new boyfriend, Sheriff Kemp, had shared privileged information, she'd added, "I just hope J.D. stays dead long enough for me to buy that new fryer I've been wanting. I'm making a mint. So's Jack Hodges over at the motor lodge."

"Consider it all payment for the strawberry-rhubarb pie recipe," Susannah had joked.

But it wasn't funny. So many fans loved J.D.'s music. And now the story about Sandy had broken, too. Apparently some journalist had gotten one of the officers from Bayou Blair to talk. On the upside, what had happened to Sandy had called national attention to the plight of many returning war veterans, and the issue of post-traumatic stress, and so Sandy was finally getting the help she needed.

Still, everyone was convinced J.D. was alive, and that he'd gone into hiding because someone was trying to kill him. Or her, since Susannah had been a target. Which meant the media was portraying J.D. as a model husband—totally self-sacrificing and willing to do anything to save his wife's life. It was enough to make Susannah blow a gasket. "A model husband," she huffed out loud, thinking about how close she'd come to being killed.

"Susannah!"

Heaving a sigh, she shoved a dish towel into the pocket of the chef's apron she wore over a white blouse and jeans. Then she scurried out to see the commotion. Joe and Tara were stuck to each other like glue, of course. The only thing unusual was that they weren't kissing. Shoot, they had started a relationship that promised to be almost as sizzling as Susannah and J.D.'s.

Sometimes Susannah would catch her best friend's gaze flickering over the new couple with envy, at least when Ellie wasn't working herself to death to keep her mind off Robby. "Why didn't you let Robby come that night you went to Joe's, Ellie?" Susannah had asked.

"I never want to see him again," Ellie vowed, but it was a lie. Ellie had loved Robby Robriquet, just as Susannah had loved J.D. So at least once a day, the two women would sit down together and share a cry.

"Remember the time we decided to leave J.D. and Robby?" Ellie had asked rhetorically. Susannah nodded, and Ellie continued, saying, "It was the smartest thing we could have done, wasn't it? I mean, what's happened since just proves it, right?"

"Absolutely," Susannah had agreed, wondering how things were going to work out once she started splitting her own time between the restaurant and Banner Manor, which she missed with all her heart.

Sighing, Susannah now followed Ellie's gaze to the TV—and gasped. "J.D." She felt a rush of temper she didn't want to examine. Her eyes dropped over the image of him critically, from the black curls glistening under a tawny Stetson, to the pearl-buttoned Western-style shirt and worn jeans. She'd gotten him the hand-tooled leather belt with a turquoise buckle for Christmas two years before.

"He's at Rockefeller Center," Ellie explained in a whisper. "At NBC."

Just fifty blocks away. Susannah gaped at the screen, warring emotions vying for control. "What's he up to now?" she muttered, watching a brunette in a pinstriped suit lean forward intently to interview him—she was closer than necessary, Susannah thought. "Who's that?"

"Lindy Montgomery," Ellie supplied in a hushed voice. "You know. She does the midday show."

"No clue," Susannah huffed. She didn't watch much TV, and lately, she'd been too preoccupied to care.

"I've been in touch with Sandy Smithers's family," J.D. was saying. "She's getting the help she needs now, and she's in all our prayers."

"And you knew Joel Murray?"

"Yes. I'm grieved by his passing, as are many people in the music industry."

It wasn't strictly true, but still, Susannah thought it was sweet of J.D. to say so.

The interviewer continued. "And this is why you kept out of the public eye?"

J.D. hesitated. "Partly."

"And to protect your wife?"

He looked toward the camera. For a long moment, he stared into the eye of the lens, as if wondering whether Susannah were watching. "Yes." That marvelous voice of his, so rich with texture and the promise of sexuality, wavered however slightly. "I could never risk having anything happen to her."

"But you're not together? Sources say you're divorcing?"

"That's right, Lindy." He turned his attention to the interviewer. "We've been estranged for quite some time."

"What happened?"

He offered the trademark cryptic J. D. Johnson smile, his glance rueful. "She loves me, but she can't live with me."

"And has your fame caused that?"

"Partly," he said again. "So you can see why the heart's

gone from my music. That's why I wanted to come on your show today. I'm changing my path."

"How so?"

"I just need to take time off, and think about how fame and fortune can change a man's life, but not always for the better."

"But you just had a big award win. You remain one of the favorites on the country music circuit and on the charts. Do you want to tell us about your next CD?"

"There's not going to be one."

Susannah's jaw slackened. Her hands flew to her hips and she glared at the screen. "What!"

"There comes a time," J.D. drawled, "when a man knows it's time for him to go. I love singing, but I don't much like the road."

The interviewer looked shocked. "But your fans?"

"I lost my biggest fan," he said. "My wife."

He was blaming her again! Susannah's hands left her hips, and she crossed her arms over her chest. Her head shook swiftly as she stared from Ellie to Joe to Tara. "Can you believe him? It's bad enough he has to break my heart," she muttered. "But now he has to break the hearts of fans."

She realized Ellie was studying her. "Well, you'd better go set him straight, Susannah."

"Somebody should! I mean, if he wants a divorce, that's fine, but he can't blame me for his career choices. That's just not fair," she said.

And a second later, she was charging through the front door of Oh Susannah's.

J.D. STEPPED TO THE SIDEWALK, unsure what he was feeling. Sadness. Heartbreak. Relief. Vertigo. "Freedom," he whispered. That was the main thing. He'd just rid himself of the source of so much of his pain. Music. To hell with it.

Taking a deep breath, he puffed his cheeks and exhaled, not bothering to fight the image of Susannah as she'd walked away that filled his mind.

She'd left his insides hollowed out and empty. Food would never taste the same. Lovemaking would never feel so passionate. His main reason for living was gone. The source of his inspiration. His muse. How could he have explained that during the interview? Without Susannah, there was no music.

And now he wanted rid of anything that had brought pain into Susannah's life, even the music, itself. He'd felt that ever since the night the *Alabama* had exploded.

Susannah had been right about everything. As soon as fame and fortune had come knocking, he'd lost his head. How many birthdays had he forgotten? How many nights had been wasted on the road...nights he and Susannah could have spent together?

But it was too late now.

Every day, he saw Susannah's eyes as she'd said goodbye, and the lost promise would haunt him forever. Love was the only thing on earth worth having. Trouble was, you never knew that until you'd lost it. He dug a pair of sunglasses from his shirt pocket and slipped them on. Tilting down the brim of his hat, he tried to focus no farther away than the dark lenses. Thanks to the interview, some people on the street were starting to recognize him.

As always, his mind had been entirely on Susannah. She was probably at her restaurant downtown, but he wouldn't bother her. She needed to get on with her life. Still, that knowledge didn't stop something gritty from stinging his eyes, and as he blinked back what might have been the beginning of tears, he was doubly glad he had on the glasses.

He start to move, but had no direction. As far back as he could remember, Susannah had been his weathervane and compass. He didn't even have a home. Banner Manor, which he loved, rightfully belonged to her.

Suddenly he turned, sensing commotion. Before he could locate the source, a familiar voice came from nowhere. "Just because we're getting a divorce doesn't mean you can quit your job, J.D.!"

"Susannah?"

She was charging toward him, swiping her hands down a chef's apron, which she wore over jeans, as if she'd run out of her restaurant without thinking. Coming to an abrupt halt in front of him, she stamped her foot, her arms crossing over her chest. "And quit looking at me like that, Jeremiah Dashiell!" she snarled.

He merely stared. Especially since she was so gorgeous. Like an angel who'd just come down from heaven. Every time he looked at her, he felt as if he'd just turned a corner and run into a world-class work of art. But what was she doing here? "Look at you like what?"

"Like you don't even know who I am although you've known me since I was five years old."

His heart was doing wild flip-flops, but he didn't dare to hope. Trying to keep his cool, he crossed his arms over his chest, and surveyed her critically. "I'm beginning to wonder if I do," he drawled slowly. "Because I thought you're the woman I'm divorcing."

Her jaw slackened. "*You're* divorcing *me!* I think you have that sentence turned around, J.D.!"

Lifting his hat by the brim, he held it in his hand and studied the band for a moment. Then he replaced the hat and looked at her again, glad for the glasses since he didn't trust his eyes not to give away his emotions. He tried to sound dumbfounded, which was easy, since he was.

"A divorce is what you want, isn't it?"

"No," she countered, her lips pursed, her chest heaving and her cheeks red, probably from the exertion of getting uptown. "What I want is for you to…to…"

He arched an eyebrow. "To?"

Tears welled in her eyes. "Oh, damn you, Jeremiah Dashiell Johnson," she burst out, stamping her foot once more. "I want you to be happy. And you can't do that without playing music, which both of us know. You're like a lost puppy every time you put down your guitar.

"But now you're trying to torture yourself because you feel guilty about everything that's happened. And as if that's not enough, you're also trying to make me feel guilty so I'll take you back."

She was right, of course. He fought to find his voice, but it stuck in his throat. "I screwed up our lives. Maybe by telling the world, other people can learn from my mistakes."

She was crying now in earnest and he couldn't stand to watch her. But he couldn't touch her, either. That might make her angrier and she'd leave, and well, he didn't want her to leave. So he just stood there, as stiff as a board, watching crocodile tears roll down her cheeks. Finally he said, "Don't you want other people to learn from my mistakes?"

"No!" she exclaimed, as if to say he were the most stupid man in the world. "I want *you* to learn from your own mistakes, J.D."

Vaguely, he was aware that a crowd was starting to form around them, but he wasn't about to let anyone come between him and Susannah ever again. Risking it, he reached and grabbed her hand, then urged her down the street. If memory served, there was a hotel on the corner. He didn't say a word until they reached it, and then he pulled her inside the door.

The doorman seemed to recognize him, and waved, indicating that he'd made sure no one followed. A clerk stepped forward, too, as if sensing the urgency, and he simply slipped J.D. a key.

"We can settle accounts later, Mr. Johnson," he said. "This way. Private elevator to the top floor."

A moment later, he and Susannah were alone heading up to their room. He slid his arms around her waist, holding her tightly.

"See. It looks like you're not really giving up the VIP treatment," she whispered.

"Some things are necessary."

She glanced up into his eyes. "This is necessary?"

Angling his head downward, he tilted his chin and brushed his lips across hers. "Very necessary," he murmured, his heart still pounding, his mind reeling with possibilities. But he didn't dare to hope. He leaned away a fraction, to stare deeply into her eyes, but he was no mind reader. Once more, he could barely find the voice that usually served him so well. "Why are you here, Susannah," he asked gently.

Her eyes were still shimmering with tears. "When I heard you on TV, I knew you were serious about not playing anymore. That's when I knew you were ready."

"Ready?"

"To truly have a life together." She paused, her voice catching. "To put me first. And our family…"

A hand moved to her belly and he gasped. "A baby…"

She shook her head. "Oh, I don't know, J.D. But let's just say I've had my first premonition." She smiled, making his heart thunder at the desire sparking in her eyes.

He was still in shock. "You're coming back to me?"

"On one condition."

"Anything."

"You keep playing music."

His breath caught. Seconds ago, he'd thought he was giving up everything, but now he knew it would all come back to him, tenfold. "Why?"

"Because you love it. And you'll put us first this time."

She was right. "I will," he promised, feathering butterfly kisses across her jaw.

She smiled. "And you need me. You need somebody who cares about all the other parts of you, the man you really are." She paused. "Now where exactly are you taking me?"

He lifted the key.

"Mama Ambrosia said a golden key would figure in my future," she whispered.

He drew her closer, burying his lips in her hair. "Sounds as if you're starting to believe in the supernatural."

"If you can change, J.D.," she murmured, her words landing against his cheek, along with kisses. "Then I guess anything's possible."

"When I…thought I could lose you, I…"

She pressed a finger to his lips. "You've got a way with words, J.D., and you write good songs, but I'm the one woman who always leaves you tongue-tied, so why don't we just wait until we get someplace quiet, where you can tell me how you feel without words?"

As if on cue, the elevator doors opened directly onto a foyer. He opened the door to the penthouse suite and pulled her into the room, heading straight for the master bedroom. "Let's kiss and make up," he agreed. "And then I'll make you as mad as a hornet."

"Why's that?"

"So we can kiss and make up again."

Quickly, they began undressing each other, their hungry

hands undoing ties and opening buttons. "I've changed, Susannah," he said as he stepped from his jeans and pulled her against him. His mouth found hers, and he delivered a slow lazy kiss, then trailed his lips down her neck. After that, he stood back, his gaze smoky as it roved over her, assessing what he was about to claim.

Suddenly, his fingers touched the charm around her neck, the one that was identical to Ellie's, and he thought about Robby's friendship, which he'd lost. But who knew? Maybe Robby would have a change of heart, too.

"Remember the time," he mused, shaking his head, his eyes meeting hers. "I won't forget again, Susannah." They'd shared so much history together, so much chemistry. And he'd almost thrown it all away. He dropped his hands, molding curves he'd feared he'd never touch again. "I feel like I've died and gone to heaven."

"Well, since my husband's decided to reincarnate," she whispered, "what about some magic? A touch of the wand? A little bayou voodoo?"

"Things are going to be different in the future," he said huskily.

"I hope not the magic."

He shook his head. "No, not the magic."

"Then what are we waiting for, J.D.?" she asked, her voice a soft rasp as she pulled him onto the bed. "It looks like high noon to me, cowboy."

"You're right. Time's a'wastin', oh, Susannah," he whispered back, settling on top of her, his body sinking into the delicious flesh he knew as well as his own, his lips silent, but his heart singing since he knew they'd never part again. "Our future starts now."

* * * * *

Celebrate 60 years of pure reading pleasure
with Harlequin® Books!

Harlequin Romance® is celebrating by showering
you with DIAMOND BRIDES in February 2009.
Six stories that promise to bring a touch
of sparkle to your life,
with diamond proposals and dazzling weddings,
sparkling brides and gorgeous grooms!

Enjoy a sneak peek at Caroline Anderson's
TWO LITTLE MIRACLES,
available February 2009
from Harlequin Romance®.

'I've found her.'

Max froze.

It was what he'd been waiting for since June, but now—now he was almost afraid to voice the question. His heart stalling, he leaned slowly back in his chair and scoured the investigator's face for clues. 'Where?' he asked, and his voice sounded rough and unused, like a rusty hinge.

'In Suffolk. She's living in a cottage.'

Living. His heart crashed back to life, and he sucked in a long, slow breath. All these months he'd feared—

'Is she well?'

'Yes, she's well.'

He had to force himself to ask the next question. 'Alone?'

The man paused. 'No. The cottage belongs to a man called John Blake. He's working away at the moment, but he comes and goes.'

God. He felt sick. So sick he hardly registered the next few words, but then gradually they sank in. 'She's got *what?*'

'Babies. Twin girls. They're eight months old.'

'Eight—' he echoed under his breath. 'They must be his.'

He was thinking out loud, but the P.I. heard and corrected him.

'Apparently not. I gather they're hers. She's been there since mid-January last year, and they were born during the summer—June, the woman in the post office thought. She was more than helpful. I think there's been a certain amount of speculation about their relationship.'

He'd just bet there had. God, he was going to kill her. Or Blake. Maybe both of them.

'Of course, looking at the dates, she was presumably pregnant when she left you, so they could be yours, or she could have been having an affair with this Blake character before...'

He glared at the unfortunate P.I. 'Just stick to your job. I can do the math,' he snapped, swallowing the unpalatable possibility that she'd been unfaithful to him before she'd left. 'Where is she? I want the address.'

'It's all in here,' the man said, sliding a large envelope across the desk to him. 'With my invoice.'

'I'll get it seen to. Thank you.'

'If there's anything else you need, Mr Gallagher, any further information—'

'I'll be in touch.'

'The woman in the post office told me Blake was away at the moment, if that helps,' he added quietly, and opened the door.

Max stared down at the envelope, hardly daring to open it, but when the door clicked softly shut behind the P.I., he eased up the flap, tipped it and felt his breath jam in his throat as the photos spilled out over the desk.

Oh, lord, she looked gorgeous. Different, though. It took him a moment to recognise her, because she'd grown her hair, and it was tied back in a ponytail, making her look younger and somehow freer. The blond highlights were gone, and it was back to its natural soft golden-brown, with a little curl in the end of the ponytail that he wanted to thread his finger through and tug, just gently, to draw her back to him.

Crazy. She'd put on a little weight, but it suited her. She looked well and happy and beautiful, but oddly, considering how desperate he'd been for news of her for the past year—one year, three weeks and two days, to be exact—it wasn't only Julia who held his attention after the initial shock. It was the babies sitting side by side in a supermarket trolley. Two identical and absolutely beautiful little girls.

* * * * *

When Max Gallagher hires a P.I. to find his estranged wife, Julia, he discovers she's not alone—she has twin baby girls, and they might be his. Now workaholic Max has just two weeks to prove that he can be a wonderful husband and father to the family he wants to treasure.

Look for TWO LITTLE MIRACLES
by Caroline Anderson,
available February 2009
from Harlequin Romance®

CELEBRATE
60 YEARS
OF PURE READING PLEASURE
WITH **HARLEQUIN®**!

**We'll be spotlighting a different series
every month throughout 2009
to celebrate our 60th anniversary.**

Look for Harlequin® Romance in February!

**Harlequin® Romance is celebrating by showering
you with Diamond Brides in February 2009.**

Six stories that promise to bring a touch of sparkle to
your life, with diamond proposals and dazzling weddings,
sparkling brides and gorgeous grooms!

Collect all six books in February 2009,
featuring *Two Little Miracles* by Caroline Anderson.

*Look for the Diamond Brides miniseries
in February 2009!*

www.eHarlequin.com   HRBRIDES09

HARLEQUIN® *Romance*®

This February the Harlequin® Romance series
will feature six Diamond Brides stories featuring
diamond proposals and gorgeous grooms.

Share your dream wedding proposal and you could WIN!

The most romantic entry will win a diamond
necklace and will inspire a proposal in one of
our upcoming Diamond Grooms books in 2010.

In 100 words or less, tell us the most romantic
way that you dream of being proposed to.

For more information, and to enter
the Diamond Brides Proposal contest, please visit
www.DiamondBridesProposal.com

Or mail your entry to us at:
IN THE U.S.: 3010 Walden Ave., P.O. Box 9069, Buffalo, NY 14269-9069
IN CANADA: 225 Duncan Mill Road, Don Mills, ON M3B 3K9

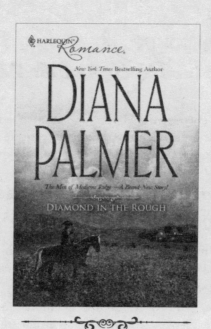

DIAMOND IN THE ROUGH

John Callister is a millionaire rancher, yet when he meets
lovely Sassy Peale and she thinks he's a cowboy, he goes along
with her misconception. He's had enough of gold diggers,
and this is a chance to be valued for himself, not his money.
But when Sassy finds out the truth, she feels John was merely
playing with her. John will have to convince her that he's truly
the man she fell in love with—a diamond in the rough.

THE MEN OF MEDICINE RIDGE—a brand-new miniseries
set in the wilds of Montana!

Available April 2009 wherever you buy books.

You're invited to join our Tell Harlequin Reader Panel!

By joining our new reader panel you will:

- Receive Harlequin® books—they are FREE and yours to keep with no obligation to purchase anything!
- Participate in fun online surveys
- Exchange opinions and ideas with women just like you
- Have a say in our new book ideas and help us publish the best in women's fiction

In addition, you will have a chance to win great prizes and receive special gifts! See Web site for details. Some conditions apply. Space is limited.

To join, visit us at
www.TellHarlequin.com.

REQUEST YOUR FREE BOOKS!

2 FREE NOVELS PLUS 2 FREE GIFTS!

HARLEQUIN®

Blaze™

Red-hot reads!

COMING NEXT MONTH

#447 BLAZING BEDTIME STORIES Kimberly Raye, Leslie Kelly, Rhonda Nelson
Who said fairy tales are just for kids? Three intrepid Blaze heroines decide to take a break from reality—and discover, to their personal satisfaction, just how sexy happily-ever-afters can be....

#448 SOMETHING WICKED Julie Leto
Josie Vargas has always believed in love at first sight—and once she meets lawman Rick Fernandez, she's a goner. If only he didn't have those demons stalking her....

#449 THE CONCUBINE Jade Lee
Blaze Historicals
Chen Ji Yue has the chance to bring the ultimate honor to her family if she is chosen as one of the new emperor's wives. Of course, first she has to beat out the other three hundred virgins vying for the position. And then she has to stay out of the bed of Sun Bo Tao, the emperor's best friend.

#450 SHE THINKS HER EX IS SEXY... Joanne Rock
24 Hours: Lost
After a very public quarrel with her boyfriend, rock star Romeo Jinks, actress Shannon Leigh just wants to get her life back. But when she finds herself stranded in the Sonoran Desert with her ex, she learns that great sex can make breaking up hard to do.

#451 ABLE-BODIED Karen Foley
Uniformly Hot!
Delta Force operator Ransom Bennett is used to handling anything that comes his way. But debilitating headaches have put him almost out of action. Luckily, his new neighbor, Hannah Hartwell, knows how to handle his pain...and him, too.

#452 UNDER THE INFLUENCE Nancy Warren
Forbidden Fantasies
Sexy bartender Johnny Santini mixes one wicked martini. Or so business exec Natalie Fanshaw discovers, sitting at his bar one lonely Valentine's night. Could a fling with him be a recipe for disaster? Well, she could always claim to be under the influence....